P9-DWR-294

F   Namioka, Lensey.
Nam   Ties that bind, ties that
              break : a novel

TIES THAT BIND,

❖

TIES THAT BREAK

TIES
THAT
BIND,

TIES
THAT
BREAK

a novel by
Lensey Namioka

DELACORTE PRESS

To the memory of my mother,
whose name, Buwei,
means "Giant Step,"
because she was one of
the earliest to have unbound feet

Published by Delacorte Press
a division of Random House, Inc.
1540 Broadway
New York, New York 10036

Copyright © 1999 by Lensey Namioka

All rights reserved. No part of this book may be reproduced or transmitted in any form or by any means, electronic or mechanical, including photocopying, recording, or by any information storage and retrieval system, without the written permission of the Publisher, except where permitted by law.

The trademark Delacorte Press® is registered in the U.S. Patent and Trademark Office and in other countries.

Library of Congress Cataloging-in-Publication Data
Namioka, Lensey.
    Ties That Bind, Ties That Break / Lensey Namioka.
    p.   cm.
    Summary: Ailin's life takes a different turn when she defies the traditions of upper-class Chinese society by refusing to have her feet bound.
    ISBN 0-385-32666-1
    [1. China—Fiction. 2. Footbinding—Fiction. 3. Sex role—Fiction. 4. Individuality—Fiction.] I. Title.
PZ7.N1426Ei   1999
[Fic]—DC21   98-27877
                                                      CIP
                                                       AC

The text of this book is set in 12-point Adobe Berling Roman.
Book design by Vikki Sheatsley
Calligraphy by Saho Fujii

Manufactured in the United States of America
June 1999
10 9 8 7 6 5 4 3 2 1
BVG

PROLOGUE

I found it hard to manage my high-heeled shoes without tripping or twisting my ankle. Wearing them was almost as bad as having bound feet. No, that wasn't true. Nothing could be as bad as having bound feet.

I also had to remember to take small steps so as not to enlarge the side slits in my silk cheong-sam. After several years of wearing a full skirt, it wasn't easy getting used to this narrow, slinky dress. The cheongsam, with its high, stiff collar and side buttons, was actually based on the Man-chu tunic Chinese women used to wear over their trousers before the Revolution. But this was 1925, and women nowadays wore only long silk stock-ings under the tunic instead of trousers, and the tunic itself fitted the body much more tightly.

Grandmother would have had hysterics if she had seen me in this outfit.

I was only nineteen, but I chose to wear the cheongsam and the high heels because I was the wife of the proprietor, and I had my dignity to maintain. As usual, I looked around the restaurant, checking to see that everything was running smoothly.

That was when I saw him.

The face was familiar, but the figure and the clothing were not. I stared at the young Chinese man dressed in a Western suit who had come into the restaurant and was looking around. There could be no doubt about it. Those raised eyebrows belonged to Liu Hanwei, my former fiancé. A huge bubble of laughter rose in my throat, and I wanted to shout a greeting.

But I had to restrain myself. Otherwise I might lose the respect of the waiters, who were all older than I was.

I walked up to Hanwei. "Would you care to sit down?" I asked politely in Mandarin. It had been three years since I had left China, but I still remembered my Chinese.

Hanwei almost jumped in surprise. He opened and closed his mouth several times. That, too, was familiar. "Ailin?" he whispered. "Are you really Tao Ailin?"

"I'm now Mrs. Zhao," I said, giving him the Mandarin form of my married name. "My husband owns this restaurant."

Stunned, Hanwei sank into the nearest chair. "You're married?" he croaked.

I nodded. I summoned a waiter, who ran over quickly. I gave him orders in rapid Cantonese. "We'll start with some shark fin soup—add some bits of chicken and ham. Then half a roast duck, I think, and some prawns in ginger sauce. Maybe a steamed carp, too."

If the waiter was surprised by the lavish order for just one guest, he refrained from commenting. Even though I was not much older than his daughter, I was still the owner's wife.

"When your employers returned to Nanjing, I went to see if you had returned with them," said Hanwei. "Imagine my shock when they told me you were staying on in America!"

I poured a cup of tea for him. "The Warners didn't need me as a nanny anymore. Both children were old enough to attend school in Nanjing."

Hanwei drank his tea silently. "But you could have found work with another American missionary family," he said finally. "Lots of them would be glad to have a fluent English speaker to care for their children."

"Maybe I got tired of being a nanny," I said lightly. Actually, that wasn't true. I loved children, and enjoyed taking care of them. "Anyway, tell me about yourself. What are you doing here in America?"

He explained that he had been studying at the University of Illinois for more than three years.

"I'm majoring in chemistry, and I'll graduate the year after next."

"If you're still studying in Illinois, what are you doing in San Francisco?" I asked.

"I was on my way home for a visit," replied Hanwei. "I heard my mother was very sick."

At the mention of his mother, Mrs. Liu, I felt a touch of bitterness. She was the one who had broken my engagement to Hanwei. But my bitterness didn't go deep.

"I have a few days to kill before my ship sails," explained Hanwei. "The University of Illinois is in a small college town without a good Chinese restaurant, and I really missed Chinese cooking. So when I was passing through San Francisco, I thought I'd drop into Chinatown for some good food." He paused, and then said softly, "The last thing I expected was to run into you!"

There was a pause. To break the heavy silence, I asked, "What do you plan to do when you graduate? Will you go back to China and find work?"

He nodded. "Yes, I already have a job waiting for me. There is a great need in China for people with technical knowledge."

The experience had been good for him, I thought. Hanwei was no longer the soft, spoiled son of a wealthy family. He was a young man ready to apply himself to a job. "Your parents will be really surprised at the change in you," I said.

The soup arrived, and Hanwei's eyes brightened when I ladled some into a bowl for him. The other dishes followed quickly, and he became too busy to talk. I had to suppress a smile as I watched him digging in. At times he didn't even wait for me to serve him but reached into the platters himself. He must have been really starved for Chinese food.

Eventually Hanwei slowed in his eating and began to pick at the bits of carp near the bones. "Not only did *I* change," he said, "but my *parents* have changed, too. You'd be surprised at how modern they've become in some respects."

"Modern enough to accept unbound feet?" I couldn't help asking.

Hanwei carefully put down his chopsticks. He stared for some moments at his teacup before replying. When he finally looked up at me, I saw that his eyes were full of sorrow and regret. "Why didn't you wait, Ailin? What made you run away to that American family?"

What made me run away? I thought back to the first time I met Hanwei. Yes, that was when it all started. I was almost five years old, and he was seven.

CHAPTER
ONE

Our family, the Taos, lived in a compound with more than fifty rooms, all surrounded by a wall. Grandfather was head of the family, and he had two sons, Big Uncle and my father. Both of them lived there with their wives and children and their own servants. Each family had a set of rooms grouped around a courtyard. Although I spent most of the time in our own rooms with my parents, my two elder sisters, and my little brother, I often visited other courtyards.

When I was a baby, my wet nurse had been a sturdy woman from the country who had lost her own baby and had milk to spare. I had a dim memory of sucking at her breast and listening to her croon lullabies. Even after I was too old to nurse, I loved to climb up on her broad lap and listen to her tell stories. I noticed that she spoke differently from the other people in our household. She was sent away when I was four, and there were times when I desperately missed her kindly face, her warm embrace, and her lilting country accent.

My parents hired an amah, or governess, to replace her. My amah spoke in a soft, ladylike manner, but she had hard eyes that never missed a single thing. I hated her constant teaching and corrections, and I tried to annoy her by talking back, using my old wet nurse's accent.

An even better way of annoying my amah was to run and hide when she called me. This was exactly what I was doing on the day when I first met my fiancé. At the time I was not quite five years old, but because my amah had bound feet, I could run a lot faster and I didn't have any trouble escaping from her. I skipped through the round gates that led from one courtyard to another.

I found a fragrant sweet-olive bush to crouch behind, and stifled my giggles as I heard my amah calling, "*San Xiaojie!* Little Miss Three!" Soon her voice lost its usual oily smoothness and became shrill.

Then I heard another voice. "Ailin, we're having moon cakes," said Second Sister. "Grandmother is entertaining guests in her room."

Moon cakes! I loved those little, rich, round cakes filled with sweet bean paste, nuts, lotus seeds, and other good things. I poked my head out from the bush. "Here I am! I bet I could stay here for a *month* without being found."

Second Sister laughed, but my amah was not amused. She seized my wrist in a grip that hurt, but loosened it when I winced. I knew she would think of some way to punish me later, but not while Second Sister was watching.

"Who are Grandmother's guests?" I asked as we hurried through two gates on our way to the courtyard where my grandparents lived.

"Young Mrs. Liu and her son," said Second Sister. She stopped and looked at me. "Your collar is buttoned wrong. You're supposed to look your best, Grandmother said."

"Why do I have to look my best?" I demanded. My amah undid the top button of my collar and pushed it through its proper loop.

Second Sister smiled. "Since Eldest Sister and I are all fixed up, it's your turn now." She wet a finger and used it to wipe away a smudge on my cheek.

"I don't understand," I said. "What do you mean by being all fixed up?"

"She means that their marriages have been arranged," my amah said with a smirk. "So it's time for Little Miss Three's marriage to be arranged, too."

"Mind you, I think you're still too young," said Second Sister. "You're not quite five."

I couldn't help grinning at Second Sister, who was only thirteen but stood smoothing her hair and trying to look like a grown-up. Maybe she hoped people would mistake her for Grandmother.

不
要
纏
足

"It's never too early to have your marriage settled," said my amah. "Some babies are engaged before they're even born."

I laughed. "They can't do that! What if the babies turn out to be both girls, or both boys?" I wasn't quite sure what a marriage meant, but I did know that it involved one of each kind, not two boys or two girls.

"Don't be stupid," snapped my amah. She stopped, and said more quietly, "Of course the families would cancel the engagement if both babies turned out to be of the same sex."

"Come on, we'd better hurry," said Second Sister, "or Grandmother will get mad."

Always happy to visit Grandmother, I immediately ran on ahead. Every now and then, I stopped and waited impatiently for my amah and Second Sister. They followed more slowly, swaying gently and taking small, mincing steps because of their bound feet.

At the entrance to Grandmother's room, my amah bowed and left as Second Sister and I entered and greeted Grandmother.

"Come in, come in," said Grandmother impatiently. "What took you so long?" She turned to the guests. "These two silly scamps are my granddaughters, and their only aim in life is to make my old age miserable."

I wasn't fooled by Grandmother's crusty manner. I knew she would let me get away with almost anything. Grandfather was a little more frightening, but he spent all his time in his study reading dusty books, so I didn't have to see much of him. The only grown-up who really scared me was Big Uncle, Father's eldest brother. He and Father spent a lot of time together, and Big Uncle was always criticizing little girls who were too fresh.

Grandmother wore her usual long satin tunic over trousers, and on her head she wore her black velvet headband decorated with pieces of carved jade. The guests were a lady and a boy who looked somewhat older than I was, maybe seven or eight years old. The lady was elegantly dressed in one of the new fashions that some of my cousins' wives were wearing. It consisted of a silk hip-length tunic worn over a skirt reaching to the ankles. Grandmother always said that women's wearing skirts was a scandalous custom adopted from the foreigners.

I waited to see if Grandmother would criticize our guest, but she showed no sign of disapproval.

The lady smiled and nodded at us. "You can't fool me, Auntie Tao! I already know that Second Sister is an accomplished young lady who plays the flute and embroiders beautifully."

"Not much wrong with Second Sister," admitted Grandmother. "It's this little one who drives me mad. Look at her! Almost five years old, and still running around like a boy."

Mrs. Liu turned and stared at me. She was smiling, but her narrowed eyes seemed to miss very little. "She looks very healthy. I'm sure she'll grow up to be a famous beauty, just like her grandmother."

不
要
纏
足

Grandmother snorted. "What nonsense! She doesn't stay still long enough to grow up, much less become a beauty."

Mrs. Liu continued to study me carefully until I felt like squirming. When her eyes reached my feet, she gave a start. "You haven't had her feet bound yet?"

Grandmother seemed embarrassed. "I've been too indulgent, I know. Every time I bring the matter up, my son finds some excuse or another to put it off."

There was a silence. Without knowing the reason for it, I could sense that something was wrong. Finally Mrs. Liu spoke. "Once the girl's feet are bound, Auntie Tao, she will stop running around. She will have time for ladylike pursuits such as embroidering."

Embroidering! I couldn't think of anything worse than sitting on a stool for hours and hours like my sisters, poking a needle through a piece of cloth. As for stopping me from running around . . .

I forgot about embroidering when two of Grandmother's maids came in with refreshments. They poured tea into delicate china cups for the grownups. Second Sister was counted as one of the grown-ups, and I could tell from her smile that she was very pleased. She picked up her cup in a prim manner and took a dainty swallow. The tea was too hot for her, and she sputtered. I had to smother a giggle.

"Delicious tea," murmured Mrs. Liu. "Everybody knows that nothing but the best Dragon Well tea is served at your house, Auntie Tao."

"You're a terrible flatterer, Mrs. Liu," said Grandmother. "Of course I gave orders to the tea merchant that he is to send us tea made only from leaves picked early in the morning, before dawn."

I was bored by the discussion of tea, and concentrated instead on the big plate of glistening brown moon cakes, which were the size of my mouth if I opened it really, really wide. Once, I had tried to cram a whole cake into my mouth and nearly choked. Now I knew that the only way to eat these rich cakes was to take small bites.

From just looking at the outside of the cakes, it was hard to tell which ones contained my favorite filling, the one with a duck-egg yolk. But I didn't get a chance to pick the one I wanted, anyway. Grandmother gave me and the Liu boy each a cake and told us to be quiet and behave.

While the grown-ups chatted about a moon-viewing party, I nibbled at my cake and looked curiously at the boy. He was chubby and a bit taller than I was. What struck me about his face was that his eyebrows were a little higher up on his forehead than they are for most people. This made him look constantly surprised.

He wasn't afraid of choking, and in three large bites he finished his cake. As he licked his fingers he stared back at me.

I didn't mind his stare. I could outstare all my male cousins. After a moment I asked, "What's your name?"

"Hanwei," he said. "I'm seven years old, and you're only five, so I'm two years older."

"Are you going to school yet?" I asked. I was proud of the fact that I had started going to the family school and already knew how to write three Chinese characters.

"Of course I'm going to school!" retorted Hanwei. "In fact, I'm going to a *public* school!"

"What's a public school?" The only school I knew was the one taught at home by teachers Grandfather had hired.

"A public school is a place where you have lessons together with boys from other families," said Hanwei.

I was amazed. "Other families? Does that mean you meet boys from just about anywhere?"

"Of course not! The boys in my school are only those that can afford to pay the fee."

"It must be really exciting to go out every day and study together with boys from other families," I said wistfully.

"It's all right," said Hanwei indifferently, but I could tell he was pleased by the impression he was making. "I even eat lunch at the school with the other students."

"You mean you all eat the same thing?" In our family school, I went back to my parents' rooms for lunch, since the cook knew my likes and dislikes. My cousins, too, went back to their rooms.

"Of course we don't eat the same thing!" said Hanwei. "My servant brings over my food when it's lunchtime. The other students have their lunches brought, too. But we all sit at the same table. We can talk as much as we want during lunch—if we're not too noisy."

"I'd love to go to a public school," I said.

"You can't," said Hanwei. "You're a girl."

"I don't see why a girl can't go to an outside school!" I protested. But I did feel a touch of doubt. Already I had learned from Mother and my amah that there were certain things boys could do that girls couldn't.

"Anyway," said Hanwei, "I can teach you some of the things I study at the school, if you want. We learn science—that's about how ice melts and becomes water, and things like that."

At our family school we spent most of our time memorizing passages from the classics, even the older boys. "What else do you learn in science?" I asked, fascinated.

"We study astronomy," answered Hanwei. "That's all about the sun, the moon, and the stars." He proceeded to tell me about eclipses, how the moon got between the sun and the earth. My amah had told me that an eclipse was caused by the Heavenly Dog trying to eat up the sun, and that we had to beat gongs loudly to scare it away. Hanwei's explanation was utterly enthralling. I couldn't imagine one of my male cousins having the patience to talk to me like this. About the only thing they did was jeer at me for being a useless girl.

"Besides science, we learn English," continued Hanwei. "Some of my teachers are Big Noses, and English is the language they speak."

Big Noses were the foreign people who came from across the ocean. "What are they like, these Big Noses?" I asked.

Hanwei's brows climbed even farther as he thought. "Well, their skin gets very pink when they're hot. Also, they're quite hairy. The hair on the backs of their hands can get an inch long!" He lowered his voice. "One of my friends told me he saw a Big Nose with his sleeves rolled up. There was hair all the way up his arms!"

I shuddered. "They must be part monkey, those Big Noses. I've never seen a human with so much hair."

Hanwei shook his head. "They're human, all right. Once you get to know them, you tend to forget how funny they look. Anyway, I have to work so hard in school that I don't have time to worry about my teacher's big nose or hairy arms."

Of all the things Hanwei studied in school, I was most interested in the foreigners' language. "Can you speak this . . . this . . . English . . . even if you don't have a big nose?" I asked.

"Of course," said Hanwei. He opened and shut his mouth a few times as he prepared himself. I

smiled, because he reminded me of the golden carp
in our fishpond. Hanwei probably thought I was ad-
miring him, because he smiled back. Finally he
managed to deliver his English words, which
sounded very strange, different from anything I had
ever heard before.

I did my best to repeat them after him. I'm good
at repeating sounds, and I infuriate some of my
cousins by imitating the way they talk.

"Hey, that's not bad!" said Hanwei. "I'll teach
you some more English, if you want."

I was touched by his offer. "That's nice of you.
But why should you bother?"

"Didn't they tell you?" asked Hanwei. He
glanced over at his mother, who was still talking in a
low voice to Grandmother. Then he turned back to
me and smiled. "I'm going to be your husband one
of these days."

CHAPTER
TWO

Two days after the visit from Mrs. Liu and Hanwei, Mother told Father that I had to have my feet bound as soon as possible.

We were sitting in our courtyard, enjoying the colorful pots of bronze chrysanthemums in full bloom. I was playing with Little Brother, who was almost one year old and just learning to walk.

"Isn't she still too young?" said Father. He put down his cup of tea and turned to look at me. I was frightened by the sadness I saw in his eyes.

"She'll be five soon," said Mother. "Most girls have it done even earlier. When Mrs. Liu saw Ailin the other day, she was shocked that her feet were still unbound. She also remarked on how spirited Ailin was. In other words, she found her spoiled and uncontrollable. Having Ailin's feet bound would stop her from running around like a boy."

I looked at Little Brother, who was tottering up to a pot of chrysanthemums. In a few years he would be able to run around just like my cousins. Why was it all right for *boys* to run around but not for me?

Father sighed. "Why can't we wait a few years before deciding on the match with the Lius? I've never been keen on these early engagements." He smiled. "Our marriage wasn't arranged until you were fourteen, and it hasn't turned out so badly, has it?"

Mother didn't smile back. "I had the definite impression that unless Ailin had her feet bound, and soon, the Lius might find another girl for Hanwei. Lots of families would be eager to offer their daughters, since the Lius are so well connected." She lowered her voice. "They're also willing to have a very modest exchange of gifts. With our heavy losses from the farm's . . ."

Mother was still talking, but I didn't wait to hear any more. I ran to find Second Sister. I had to know exactly what it was like to have my feet bound, and Second Sister was the only one I could count on to tell me the truth. Mother and my amah would only say things that would make me do what they wanted.

I found Second Sister in the courtyard, looking over her tray of silkworms. The worms had already spun their cocoons, and all I could see were little fuzzy balls shaped like pigeon eggs, only smaller. "Look!" said Second Sister. "Here's one that's pale green! Too bad we don't have more of the same color. We could have beautiful green silk thread without having to dye."

Second Sister had given me some silkworm eggs once and showed me how to raise them in a tray. But I was starting the family school just then, and I forgot to feed the silkworms mulberry leaves. By the time I remembered them, they were stiff and dead.

I was so fascinated looking at Second Sister's cocoons that I almost forgot what I was going to ask. "How many of these cocoons do you need to make a beautiful jacket?"

Second Sister laughed. "I'd need hundreds— maybe thousands! I'm not raising these worms for the silk, only for a hobby." She looked at me. "What's the matter? Is something wrong?"

I glanced down at Second Sister's feet and didn't know what to say. As long as I could remember, both my sisters had had tiny, wedge-shaped feet. "How did you get your feet small enough to squeeze into those pointy shoes?" I blurted out finally.

After a long moment Second Sister sighed. "I see. Mother is talking about having your feet bound, isn't she? For you, it's almost too late. Mine were done before I was four years old."

"Did it hurt? Did you cry?"

Second Sister quickly smoothed her face, but I had already seen her grimace. "It was bad, wasn't it?" I asked, hoping desperately that Second Sister would deny it.

But she only sighed again. Then she pulled me close and stroked my cheek. "We women all have had to go through this ordeal: Mother, Grandmother, Eldest Sister, Mrs. Liu, your amah. Life is hard on women. In a few years you'll also find out that you'll be bleeding once a month."

I already knew about the monthly bleeding, since I had caught sight of my amah's bloody napkins. Then I remembered something. "Not all the women have bound feet! My wet nurse had feet like a man's, and she didn't have to hobble around." I looked up at Second Sister. "Is that why Mother sent her away? Because she had big feet?"

Second Sister laughed. "Of course not! You ask too many questions." She lowered her head and thoughtfully fingered some of her silk cocoons. Then she seemed to come to a decision. "You can come into my room tonight when I'm washing my feet. Then you'll see how I manage to squeeze my feet into my shoes."

I saw the same sorrow in Second Sister's eyes that had been in Father's. It made me so nervous that I didn't feel hungry at dinner that night.

Often, when Father had male guests for company, my sisters and I ate separately with Mother or Grandmother. Tonight Big Uncle was joining my parents for dinner, but since he counted as family, we womenfolk could eat with them.

不要纏足

不
要
纏
足

Big Uncle seemed to dislike children, especially girls. I tried to keep quiet when he was around, but sometimes I forgot myself and spoke out. Then I got the feeling that he wanted to squash me like a bedbug.

The sight of Big Uncle's stern face at the dinner table took away the rest of my appetite. He glanced at me once during the meal and then turned to Father. "Have Ailin and the Liu boy met each other yet?"

"Mrs. Liu brought her son over the day before yesterday," said Father. "They seemed to get on well enough, Mother tells me." He smiled at me. "You liked Hanwei, didn't you?"

I was too embarrassed to speak and just mumbled something.

"Speak up!" ordered Big Uncle. He rolled his eyes. "Young people can't even talk properly these days!"

It was impossible to satisfy Big Uncle. When I really spoke up, he scolded me for being too bold. And now he was scolding me for speaking too softly!

"Besides, what's the point of having those children meet, anyway?" continued Big Uncle. "My first wife and I had our first look at each other when I lifted her red bridal veil at the wedding!"

Personally, I thought that if First Auntie had seen Big Uncle's face beforehand, she would have run away screaming instead of going on with the wedding.

"Well, things are changing these days, Elder Brother," Father said soothingly. "We can't stick to the old ways forever."

"You're always talking about how things are changing!" said Big Uncle. "It's the result of your job at the customs office. You come in contact with all sorts of strange people, including foreigners, and you get strange new ideas!"

"Not all new ideas are strange," said Father.

Big Uncle frowned. "Now you sound like one of those revolutionary types! I've heard a lot of dangerous talk about toppling the empire and setting up a republic!"

"We can't shut our eyes to what's happening in the rest of the world," said Father. "For thousands of years, we called ourselves the Middle Kingdom and refused to learn from anyone outside."

"We haven't done so badly!" said Big Uncle.

"But we *have* done badly!" said Father. "We've been defeated many times by foreign powers. At the moment, we're ruled by an alien people, the Manchus."

Big Uncle looked around and lowered his usually loud voice. "Be careful of what you say. The empire may seem weak, but it still has teeth."

"Rotten teeth," said Father. I giggled, although I didn't quite get the joke.

Big Uncle frowned darkly but didn't contradict Father. I had noticed that he listened more to Father than to anyone else. I was proud of Father. His manner was mild toward everyone, but I knew he was very wise. In my eyes he was the perfect Chinese gentleman. Big Uncle, with his loud bluster, didn't fit our teacher's description of the classical ideal. I wanted to point this out every time Big Uncle went on and on about young people not paying attention to the classics. But so far I hadn't had the nerve.

"Take the Opium War of 1839," Father went on. "Losing that war forced us to hand over Hong Kong to the British."

The Opium War was such a humiliation for our country that even the teacher in our family school had told us all about it, although he had been hired to teach only the classics. He told us that the British wanted to sell opium to China, but our government refused to allow its importation, whereupon Britain went to war against us. Our defeat opened our country to the drug and made opium addicts out of thousands of our people.

"We lost the Opium War because of Governor Lin Zexu's incompetence!" growled Big Uncle.

"Lin Zexu was not incompetent," said Father. "He just didn't have the support he needed from the central government. Furthermore, his forces had no defense against the superior weapons of the British."

"Those greedy foreign devils!" spat Big Uncle. He sounded so angry that I half expected him to get up and stalk from the room. Dinner would be a lot pleasanter without him. But he just slammed his rice bowl down angrily. A maid rushed over and hurriedly refilled it.

"We don't have to reject everything brought by the foreign devils," said Father. "The Lius are pretty conservative, and they are sending their sons to a public school run by the foreigners."

Big Uncle's voice resumed its normal volume as he started a tirade on public schools and useless lessons in astronomy and trigonometry, subjects no gentleman should have to study.

I had been trying to shut my ears to Big Uncle's booming voice, but the mention of the public school caught my attention. I remembered Hanwei's telling me about his studies. If Big Uncle disliked those subjects, they were sure to be fascinating.

Thinking about Hanwei reminded me of something. "Mrs. Liu wore a skirt when she was visiting Grandma," I said brightly. "That's a foreign fashion."

"Little girls shouldn't interrupt their elders!" shouted Big Uncle. "Who wants to hear your stupid jabber about skirts and fashions?"

For a moment I was afraid he would slam his rice bowl down hard enough to crack it. We lost a lot of dishes when Big Uncle came to eat with us. Fortunately the cook chose that moment to bring out a big bowl of eight-jewel rice, which we all loved.

The sweet dish helped to soothe Big Uncle's temper, and the conversation turned to other things.

不
要
纏
足

Then the subject of imported, machine-woven cloth came up, and this made Big Uncle furious again. "Everybody is buying imported cloth, and our weavers can't sell their handwoven cloth!"

"Machine-woven cloth is cheaper," Father pointed out. "That means our poorer people can afford new clothes more often."

"*We* might become poorer people soon," said Big Uncle. "An important part of our income comes from the women and their looms on our farms, and this year it's less than a quarter of what it was last year!"

I was bored by all this talk of machine- and hand-woven cloth. My thoughts went back to the prospect of visiting Second Sister's room and watching her wash her feet. My stomach began to churn.

A family supper didn't last long, since most of the dishes were served all at once, not one at a time. There was still a little bit of daylight left in the autumn sky when we young people were dismissed, and water pipes were brought in for the grown-ups.

Out in the courtyard the huge golden ball of the autumn moon had just risen and seemed to be resting on top of the curved roof of Second Sister's room. She took me by the hand. "Come on, let's go in."

I hung back. "It's still bright enough to play outside."

"Very well, you can play outside if you want to," said Second Sister, quickly dropping my hand. She sounded relieved. "I'm not forcing you to watch anything."

I took a deep breath. I had to know. "No, I'm coming in to watch you."

Inside the room the maid was already pouring hot water into a basin. Eldest Sister was away, visiting one of her sisters-in-law. She was sixteen, and she was going to be married in two months. Since she had a lot to learn, she spent every minute she could with one of the young wives.

When the maid finished pouring the water, Second Sister sat down on a stool and began to unwrap the strips of white cotton cloth around her feet. The strips were long, and the unwrapping seemed to take forever. As one of Second Sister's feet was being uncovered, I noticed an unpleasant smell.

"Disgusting, isn't it?" said Second Sister. "The smell comes from the sweat that gets trapped in the folds of the skin."

"Don't you wash your feet every day?" I just couldn't imagine my fastidious sister with smelly feet.

Second Sister made a face. "I try to wash my feet as often as I can, but the cloth is bound so tightly that no air can reach the skin. It's especially bad in this warm weather."

When both strips of cloth were completely unwound, Second Sister stretched out her legs and placed her feet in the hot water. She gave a sigh, and I couldn't tell whether it was from pain or relief.

I stared at the pitiful stumps at the ends of Second Sister's legs. The sight made me sick. I had expected to see miniature toes at the ends of Second Sister's feet, because how else would they fit into the pointed ends of her tiny shoes?

Now I saw how her foot had been squeezed into a wedge: The big toe had been left undeformed, but the rest of the foot with the other toes had been forced down under the sole of her foot, like a piece of bread folded over. The only way the toes could have been folded over was for the bones to have been broken.

Having bound feet must have been agony for Second Sister, Eldest Sister, Mother, Grandmother, and generations of other women. What was more, they didn't suffer just for an instant. The pain must have gone on and on for weeks, months, and years.

I'll never let them do this to me, I vowed to myself. Never! Never!

CHAPTER
THREE

They came for me three days later.
I had gone to our family school early in the
morning as usual. I didn't find the schoolwork par-
ticularly hard, but it was sometimes boring. We
were working on the *Three Word Classic*, a rhymed
reader, which opened with the statement that human nature was good. The book then went on to
outline Chinese history. Although the reader was
meant for children, we couldn't understand it very
well because it had been written in the thirteenth
century and its language was very different from
ours.

As usual the teacher didn't try to explain the
meaning but just ordered us to memorize the text.
We droned on and on in unison, reciting the text
without understanding it.

Next came the part I enjoyed: brush writing. I

loved the smell as I rubbed the ink stick in the little pool of water to make a thick black ink. My cousin, Big Uncle's youngest son, spilled ink on his work sheet and tried to hide the puddle by putting his sleeve over it. Of course, that just made the mess worse. Big Uncle was so harsh toward his children that they always tried to hide whatever they did. That made them sly, which was the reason I didn't like them very much.

When school was over I played in our courtyard and watched a beetle crawling around in a pot of chrysanthemums. Mother, my amah, and two maids moved in very quietly, and I didn't hear their approach. They caught me before I had a chance to run and hide.

Mother's hands came down firmly on my shoulders. "Come on, Ailin," she said. "It's time."

"Time for what?" I asked.

As they dragged me to my room I wondered which of my misdeeds was catching up with me. Talking back in a saucy manner to the teacher in the family school? Putting an earthworm in my amah's bowl of noodles? Hiding all Eldest Sister's underclothes just when she was packing her trunks to take them to her future husband's house?

But instead of scolding me when they reached my room, Mother said in a gentle voice, "Remember, this is something we all go through. It's part of growing up."

My heart began to beat faster. I wasn't sure I

wanted to grow up. Then I saw the strips of white cloth folded neatly on my bed, and I guessed what was going to happen. "No, no!" I cried. "I don't want my feet bound!"

"It doesn't hurt," said Mother, still speaking gently. "All we're going to do is wrap your feet in the cloths. There'll be no cutting or breaking. I promise!"

I didn't believe her and continued to struggle. "Yes, you will! You'll have to break my feet to make the toes go under!"

Mother's face became rigid. "Who said your feet will be broken? The toes will be bent gradually, a bit at a time. We'll do it so slowly that you'll hardly feel it."

"It hurts! It hurts! I know it hurts!" I screamed. "I saw Second Sister's feet! You can't fool me!"

With a sudden jerk I managed to break free from the maids and run out of the room. This time I had a head start. I could run much faster than the others, since my feet were free. Through a series of moon gates I ran, weaving my way among the porcelain planters, sweet-olive bushes, and pomegranate trees. I knew a thousand hiding places that the grown-ups didn't. I could live on pomegranate seeds for days, weeks, *months*, if I had to.

The voices of my amah and the maids grew fainter. I stepped behind a planter and crouched, panting. What should I do next? Maybe I could get help from one of my cousins, Big Uncle's sons. They were boys and didn't have bound feet, so they could understand why I wanted freedom.

On the other hand, they might not want to help me. They were slow and lazy. All too often I enjoyed making fun of them by imitating their stumbling recitations and watching their faces turn purple, just as Big Uncle's face did. The two boys would be the first to betray me to the grown-ups.

Time passed. I heard the voices of the searchers pass close, but I kept completely still. I had learned by watching how sparrows kept still when a cat was near. More time passed.

Then something happened that I hadn't expected. I felt a growing pressure down below. I needed to pee! It would be easy enough to pull down my pants and do it right on the ground. But I remembered how Little Brother went around with a slit in the back of his pants and peed whenever he felt like it. A servant always came up afterward to turn the dirt, since there would be a bad smell otherwise. If I did it here behind the planter, the smell would give me away.

I began to change my hiding places, and after a while I found myself close to the compound where my parents and sisters had their rooms.

I heard voices. One was Mother's, raised in anger. "Why did you do it? Why did you show her your feet?"

There was the sharp crack of a slap. Finally Second Sister's voice said softly, "She had to learn the truth. It's more honest. I know Ailin, and I know

32

that you can't fool her. If you tried to trick her, she would never respect you again."

"Respect!" cried Mother's voice. "Children *owe* respect to their parents! We don't have to earn it!"

"But you can lose it," said Second Sister.

Another slap. I peeked out from behind the bush and saw Mother grabbing Second Sister by the hair with one hand and slapping her with the other.

I couldn't stand it any longer. "Stop!" I cried, dashing out from my hiding place and rushing toward Mother. "It's not Second Sister's fault!"

Mother froze. She dropped her arms and slowly turned. The angry red faded from her face as she looked at me.

Expecting a rain of slaps to fall on me, I covered my cheeks. But Mother only stared at me. For a long moment the three of us stood motionless. I looked at Mother's stony face, and at Second Sister's red, swollen cheeks. A great big lump of charcoal seemed to be stuck in my throat.

Mother finally broke the silence. "How can we find a decent husband for you if you refuse to have your feet bound?" she whispered. Instead of slapping me, she suddenly gathered me in her arms and held me close. "My poor little girl, you're beautiful, and you're clever. But you are too headstrong. Someday you will have to pay a price for that."

For a while there was no more talk of foot binding. The grown-ups were completely preoccupied with something that was happening outside our home. I

33

heard the word *revolution* used many times, but when I asked what it meant, Mother only shook her head. "You're too young to understand, Ailin."

My cousins in the family school told wild stories, although they didn't really know more than I did about what was happening. "*Revolution* means that everything is turned upside down!" said one cousin. "So high officials become servants, and beggars become governors."

"Does that mean students become teachers, then?" asked the other cousin.

"You'll have a chance to find out," I told him. "Because here comes our teacher."

My cousins scurried back to their seats and tried to look studious. But if the teacher had overheard our talk, he didn't give any sign. He was very distracted, and after a few scattered comments about our work, he suddenly announced that class was dismissed for the day.

Openmouthed, we stared at him as he dashed out the door and hurried through the courtyard. We never saw him again. Eventually Grandfather hired a new teacher. It wasn't until months later that I learned from Father that our teacher had been connected with the revolutionaries, and he had left Nanjing and joined some comrades in the north.

That was the closest that our family ever came to meeting an actual revolutionary. Most of the time we just tried hard to lead our normal life.

At first some of the servants refused to go out

and buy food. "It's not safe!" cried the servant girl who usually shopped for vegetables. "The government soldiers have fled, and nobody knows who is in charge."

Grandmother gave the girl a good scolding. "Stop that foolishness! Everybody still has to eat, and you'll find the market open as usual."

The girl reluctantly went to the market, and reported that things were quiet. "I wasn't scared at all!" she said, pleased by the attention she was getting from the rest of the household.

"When will you be able to go back to work?" Mother asked Father.

Father was usually at work in the customs office by the time I finished eating my breakfast, but for the past few days he had been staying home, talking quietly with Big Uncle or Grandfather. "There are few reports of looting," he said. "From what I've heard, the rebels are setting up a new government and establishing law and order. It seems that they are not all bandits or hoodlums. If things continue like this, I may be able to go back to work quite soon."

"What has happened to the emperor and his family?" asked Second Sister.

"The rumor is that they've fled from the capital," said Father. "I've heard reports that they'll seek refuge in Japan."

"Maybe one of the rebels will establish a new dynasty and make himself emperor," said Mother.

"There is talk that some of the rebels want to do away with the empire altogether and establish a republic," said Father.

"What's a republic?" I asked.

"Little children shouldn't ask stupid questions," said Mother, frowning at me.

Father smiled. "No, let her ask. In fact I'm not sure myself what the answer is to Ailin's question. A republic, as far as I know, is a state governed by the will of the people."

The answer didn't make things any clearer to me. The will of what people? People like us, or people like our servants?

"It seems strange not to have an emperor," murmured Second Sister. "For more than two thousand years our country has always had an emperor."

"Things can change," said Father. He glanced at Little Brother, who was sitting on Mother's lap, playing with her jade bracelet. "My son, you may grow up in a country without an emperor," he crooned, reaching over and tickling Little Brother under the chin.

I hoped Father was right. If things changed, maybe girls wouldn't have to have their feet bound any longer. I was all in favor of the Revolution, whatever it was.

With all the excitement over the Revolution, I thought Mother had forgotten about foot binding. I began to breathe more easily.

But my relief was premature. A summons came

from Grandmother, and this time I had to go alone.
This time there were no moon cakes, no company
to greet.

"What's this I hear about not wanting your feet
bound?" demanded Grandmother. Instead of giving
me her usual indulgent smile, she fixed me with a
stern look. Even the wrinkles around her eyes,
which had always been laughter lines, now looked
like cruel slashes.

I was facing a stranger. This was not the kindly
grandmother who always took my side when I was
in trouble. There would be no refuge for me in
Grandmother's room if I wanted to run from my
pursuers. I swallowed a few times. "I want to be
able to walk freely. I don't want to hobble around."

"*You* want this and *you* don't want that!" cried
Grandmother. "What you want and what you don't
want make no difference! You don't give orders
here, little girl! You *take* orders!"

I had never been afraid of Grandmother before. I
took a deep breath and tried to blink back the tears
that threatened to spill out. I bit my lips to prevent
them from trembling. "Father said that things are
changing because of the Revolution."

"Revolution!" cried Grandmother. "What does
that have to do with anything? People still have to
live, to marry, and to bear children! Your father
thinks things will change. Perhaps they will. But
men will always be men, and women will always be
women. Some things never change!"

不
要
纏
足

When I looked up at Grandmother's face again, her eyes were softer. "Ailin, you've already met your future husband, Hanwei."

When I nodded Grandmother went on. "You liked him, didn't you?"

I pictured Hanwei's raised eyebrows and look of surprise. I remembered the earnest way he tried to teach me English. "He's all right," I admitted. "Anyway, he's a lot better than my cousins."

Suddenly Grandmother smiled and looked like herself again. "You can do worse—much worse. Mrs. Liu told me that Hanwei liked you, too. It will be a good match, and you will be happy when you become a member of the Liu family. You can come home as often as you like because the Lius have been friends of our family for generations, and we see a lot of one another." Then her face hardened again. "But there will be no marriage unless your feet are bound! The Lius have very high standards, and they will not accept a daughter-in-law with feet like a peasant's!"

I opened my mouth, but Grandmother waved me away. "Don't bother me with excuses. I'll tell your mother I've spoken to you."

That night Mother and the maids brought the strips of cloth again, and this time I didn't try to run away. I sat quietly on the bed while they bound the strips tightly around my toes, bending all except the big toes against the soles of my feet. It was uncomfortable, but it didn't feel as bad as I had expected. Maybe Mother had told the truth after all. Foot binding was just something we women had to bear if we wanted to marry decently.

I changed my mind when I tried to get up from bed after the wrapping. Putting weight on my bound feet sent sharp stabs of pain into my bent toes, and the pain went shooting all the way up my legs.

"What are you doing?" said my amah. "You're not supposed to get up for several weeks!"

"What do you mean?" I demanded. "Why can't I get up? I'm not sick!"

Mother hurried over. "Of course it will hurt when you try to walk now, Ailin. You have to put weight on your feet very gradually. You need patience to learn how to walk on bound feet."

The phrase *learn how to walk on bound feet* was what struck me the hardest. I suddenly realized that I would never walk naturally again. I would never run laughing through the moon gates of our courtyards and hide from my cousins and the servants. For the rest of my life I would be hobbling around!

A wave of fury swept over me, and I began tearing at the cloths around my feet.

My amah rushed over, joined by two of the maids. They tried to hold me down, but I just thrashed and screamed more and more loudly.

"We may have to tie her down," said one of the maids finally.

"But we can't tie her down for weeks and weeks," objected Mother.

"She'll tear off the cloth strips when we're not

looking," said my amah. "I will have to watch her the whole time, day and night."

The thought of being continuously under the amah's eyes drove me into a frenzy. I screamed and struggled even more wildly. I bit down hard on someone's hand, and I didn't care whose it was.

"What is happening here?" said a male voice.

Father was standing at the door. The women around my bed quickly released their hands and stepped back. He walked into the room, looked down at me, and then turned to look at Mother. For a long, long time the two of them stared at each other.

Finally Father broke the silence. "Ailin doesn't have to have her feet bound if she doesn't want it."

"She's too young to understand the consequences," said Mother.

"But *I* understand the consequences," said Father. "Let her run free if that's what she wants."

I didn't understand the exchange between my parents. What did they mean by *consequences*?

In the months that followed, nothing bad seemed to be happening to me after all. Even Grandmother didn't try to scold me, although she shook her head a few times when she saw me, and sighed. That didn't bother me. I really thought my life would go on as before.

But I was wrong. The announcement came four months after it was definitely decided that my feet would not be bound. Mother stared bitterly at me as we were sitting down to dinner. "Mrs. Liu called the matchmaker today to say that her family wants to break off your engagement with Hanwei. I told you this would happen!"

Second Sister reached for my hand and gave it a reassuring squeeze, but her eyes were troubled. Although Father said nothing, I knew he was worried about my future, too.

Mother was the one who lamented loudly and frequently. "I suppose Ailin can become a nun," she said. "That's one respectable livelihood open to an unmarried woman. Of course, with her agility, she can always become an acrobat and street entertainer!"

"Be quiet!" said Father. He seldom spoke harshly to anyone. For him to use this tone with Mother—and in front of the children—meant he was greatly disturbed.

I didn't see why Father was so shocked at Mother's suggestion. I'd always wanted to run around freely in the streets, and it would be fun to entertain people. I peeked at Mother and saw that she was biting her lips, trying not to weep.

Father took a deep breath and spoke more gently. "We cannot expect our old customs to remain forever—even customs that have prevailed for a thousand years. I will think of a plan. There must be something to do for a girl with unbound feet."

CHAPTER
FOUR

Nothing was decided about my future for more than four years. Although my engagement with Hanwei was broken, we couldn't completely avoid meeting the Lius, since our social circle was a small one.

The city had quieted down, and it had become safe again for family outings. One favorite treat was boating on Lake Xuanwu on the outskirts of Nanjing. The lake had several pretty islands, as well as arched stone bridges that connected them. We rented a boat, our cook prepared a delicious picnic, and our family spent a lovely afternoon on the lake.

Near one of the islands we approached another boat. A familiar face peeked out between the curtains of the other vessel, and I recognized the high eyebrows of Liu Hanwei. When Hanwei saw me, he grinned and pulled his head back inside. Seconds later Mrs. Liu leaned out and greeted us.

By now I was old enough to realize that this was an embarrassing situation. But Mother and Mrs. Liu simply exchanged a few remarks about Second Sister's coming marriage, and after a few more polite words the two boats separated. Hanwei waved as his boat pulled away.

I waited for Mother to reproach me again about my broken engagement, but she had apparently decided it was a dead subject. These days the grown-ups had too many other things to think about.

The world was changing so much that even inside the walls of our compound we couldn't help hearing things. I was fascinated by descriptions of smoke-belching ships that came up the Yangtze River as far as Nanjing, and even beyond. I also heard about "iron roads," which were twin metal rails on which boxes on wheels could be pulled great distances by "fire cars" burning wood or coal.

Father and Big Uncle talked a great deal about the republic, our new government, and whether it would last. "I've heard rumors that Yuan Shikai might make himself emperor and start a new dynasty," said Father.

Big Uncle was all in favor of a new dynasty. "That would be an improvement over this wishy-washy republic we've got. With an emperor, we might get some stability at last. Our country needs a firm leader in control."

I pictured a firm leader in control, barking out orders. Naturally he would be someone who looked and sounded just like Big Uncle.

Both Father and Big Uncle talked a lot about the dangers of our country's being carved up by foreign powers. "Japan, Germany, and Russia are already establishing their spheres in the north," growled Big Uncle, his face turning purple, as usual when foreigners were mentioned.

Father admitted that foreigners were arriving in greater and greater numbers. "But I believe our country can also benefit from the presence of these people. There is a lot we can learn from them."

One evening, when I was nine years old, Father made an announcement. "I'm going to enroll Ailin in a public school."

Four years earlier I would have jumped up and down with excitement. I was older now and could stay put on my stool, but I couldn't prevent myself from breaking out into a big smile. Memories of what Hanwei had told me about public schools came rushing back. What had he studied? Something about eclipses, and water melting, and English, that strange language spoken by the Big Noses.

My parents, Second Sister, and I were eating supper with Grandmother. Grandfather was sick and had his usual bowl of gruel in bed. But Grandmother liked the sight of young faces around the table. Besides, having people over was an excuse to have the cook serve something fancy.

Grandmother frowned on hearing Father's announcement. "You must have taken leave of your senses! Ailin will study for another year at the family school, and that's all the education she will need. Too much studying is unhealthy for a girl!"

There was a silence. Second Sister and I exchanged glances, and I knew we were both thinking of the same thing. She had told me that Father had had an elder sister, who came between him and Big Uncle in age. She had been unusually intelligent and was an accomplished poet. Grandfather, a dedicated scholar, had personally taught her brush writing because she had shown an early talent for it. But she had died of the dreaded lung disease when she was only fifteen, even before her marriage could be arranged. Grandmother was convinced that too much studying had caused her early death.

According to Grandmother, I looked a lot like this aunt whom I had never seen. Second Sister had told me that Father was very fond of his lost sister, and maybe he wanted to give me the chance at education that his sister had not had. He refused to believe that studying was unhealthy.

Grandmother was still unconvinced. "What sort of public school would accept girls, anyway?"

"It's called the MacIntosh, and it's a public girls' school run by missionaries," said Father. "A colleague in the customs office told me he was sending his daughter there."

45

"A school run by missionaries? What are missionaries?"

"They preach their religion to people of other countries," explained Father. "The ones operating this school are American Protestants. They belong to a branch of the Christian religion."

"You're thinking of sending Ailin to a school where they preach the *Jesu* religion?" cried Grandmother. "What are you wasting money on that for?"

"The school doesn't teach the children just religion," explained Father. "The students will also study the history of the world, geography, mathematics, English, and other useful things."

Grandmother's eyes widened. "*Useful* things? I can't imagine how a well-bred girl like Ailin could possibly find the history of the world useful!"

"Our country has been isolated too long," said Father. "It's because of our ignorance that we were humiliated by the foreign powers in the disastrous Boxer Rebellion."

I remembered hearing Father and Big Uncle talk about the Boxer Rebellion, which had taken place fifteen years earlier. A band of outlaws calling themselves Boxers attacked some foreigners in Beijing, the capital city. Before the Boxers were put down, a number of foreigners had been killed.

"The Boxers were just some crazy lunatics," snapped Grandmother. "They deserved to be wiped out!"

"But in reparation our government was forced to pay enormous sums of money to those foreign countries," said Father. "Even worse, we had to give up land to the foreigners, and now there are parts of our country controlled by foreign troops. In sections of Shanghai, foreign policemen enforce *their* laws over *our* people!"

"Those foreign devils defeated us with their magic," said Grandmother. "Our brave men were no match for their big guns."

"Precisely," said Father. "So among other things, we have to learn how those big guns were developed. When the Boxers laid siege to the foreign legations in Beijing, they thought they could overwhelm the foreigners by sheer numbers. They were mowed down by those guns."

Grandmother laughed. "And you think girls like Ailin should go to a public school and learn how to make guns? Defeat foreign soldiers?"

I giggled, and even Father had to smile. "Of course not!" he said. "But we can't think of ourselves forever as the center of the universe. Ailin and young people like her have to find out about the rest of the world."

"I'm not going to argue with you about world affairs," Grandmother said, sighing. "But just think of the practical difficulties: How is Ailin going to travel to school, for instance? Of course, with her big feet she can simply walk. But that would ruin her reputation."

"Her reputation is already ruined because of her big feet," muttered Mother.

Grandmother glared at Mother, who quickly became silent. Father had the answer. "I can have the chauffeur take her in the family rickshaw."

I was delighted. I always enjoyed a ride in the rickshaw with Mother. Speed was its best feature, plus the smooth ride on its two big wheels. But I didn't often get a chance to ride the rickshaw, since Grandfather, Father, and Big Uncle—the men in the family—had first call on the vehicle for their errands.

Grandmother continued to grumble. "I never liked the rickshaw. Confounded Japanese invention! I prefer an old-fashioned sedan chair, which takes you around at a reasonable, dignified pace."

For myself, I didn't like the sedan chair because it tossed me up and down, especially when the carriers decided to give me a bouncy ride.

"What about meals?" demanded Grandmother. "Ailin would be eating with strangers. She can't digest turnips. What if the school kitchen serves great big heaps of turnips? You never know what those foreigners take it into their heads to eat!"

"I can have lunch brought to me," I said quickly. "One of the servants can carry over a stack of hot dishes and rice. All the students have their meals brought."

The grown-ups turned and stared at me. "How in heaven did you know that?" asked Mother.

"Hanwei told me," I said. "He goes to a public

school, too, and he said his lunch was brought over, things he likes to eat."

There was another long silence. Whenever Hanwei's name was mentioned, Father would look grave, Mother sad, and Grandmother furious.

Finally Grandmother threw down her chopsticks with a clatter. "Having Ailin attend school is not going to help the matchmaker. It's hard enough when the girl has big feet, but an *educated* girl with big feet will be quite impossible to marry off!"

To be accepted into the MacIntosh School, I first had to pass an entrance examination. In preparation I reviewed what I had been studying in our family school. When I was five, I had studied the *Three Word Classic*. Later I had gone on to other texts, some of them taken from the teachings of the masters such as Confucius and Mencius. All of these teachings we memorized. In fact, my schooling at home consisted of memorizing texts written in ancient Chinese.

On examination day we arrived at the school building, which was very different from the houses in our family compound. At home our compound consisted of small one- or two-room buildings grouped around courtyards. The school occupied just one huge building but had dozens of rooms. I couldn't imagine how people could walk around inside without getting lost.

But Father didn't seem surprised by the size of

the building and had no trouble finding his way to the room where I was to take the examination. A young woman invited us to sit at a table and served us tea.

A mild-looking man came in and introduced himself as an assistant headmaster. He reminded me a little of Father, and I relaxed.

Mr. Li, the examiner, started by asking me about the things I had learned in our home school. Thankful that I had done my review, I quickly recited a number of passages I had memorized.

We went on to the next part of the examination, which consisted of writing some Chinese characters. A stone slab and ink stick were brought in. I poured a few drops of water onto the slab and rubbed the stick in the water until I got a nice thick pool of black ink. Then I carefully dipped my brush and wrote the characters for *family*, *country*, and *book*. When the examiner smiled, I knew he liked my work, so I decided to write the hardest character I knew, which was the one for *virtue*. It took fifteen strokes.

Mr. Li nodded. For the first time I was grateful to our teacher in the family school, who had worked us so hard. Mr. Li then chatted with me and asked me what I hoped to learn. No adult had ever talked to me like this before.

"I want to learn about the rest of the world, not just about China," I declared. This was just repeating what Father had said earlier, but I realized that I really *was* very curious about other countries.

Suddenly I noticed that Mr. Li was looking at something behind me. A woman had quietly come into the room, and the sight of her made me catch my breath. This was my first close look at a foreigner.

Once, in the streets, I had caught a brief glimpse of a foreigner riding by in a rickshaw. My amah had whispered, "There goes one of the Big Noses!" By the time I'd turned around to get a better look, the rickshaw had whizzed by.

Now I stared at this foreign woman. True, her nose stuck out a bit more than normal, but it was not monstrously big. I couldn't see whether her arms were hairy or not, since she wore long sleeves. What I could see was the hair on her head, which was the light brown of dried pine needles. Her eyes were gray, and since they bulged a little, they looked like round pebbles in pools of clear water.

I quickly peeked at the foreign woman's feet. They were unbound. Later I would learn that no foreign women had bound feet. In the whole wide world, only Chinese women bound their feet.

Mr. Li greeted the newcomer in a language I didn't understand, and the foreign woman responded. They must have spoken in English. Then she turned to my parents and smiled. Her smile was big and white and friendly. "How do you do?" she said in Chinese. "I am Miss Gilbertson. I shall be your daughter's English teacher."

As I heard my parents returning greetings to the teacher, I realized that I had been accepted into the school.

With my entrance into the MacIntosh School, I began one of the happiest periods of my life. My studies included Chinese writing and literature but with less emphasis on simply memorizing and more on discussing the material. We also studied what Grandmother called "useless subjects." In the class called geography, I learned about other countries and other peoples, just as Father had hoped. I was fascinated to hear about people who had skins as dark as charcoal and others who lived in houses made of ice.

Although the school was run by American missionaries, most of the teachers were Chinese men, and only one class a day was spent on religion. Still, I rather enjoyed these religion classes in which we heard what the teacher called Bible stories. They were fascinating tales about ancient peoples, and my favorite was the one about a young boy who killed a ferocious giant with a weapon called a slingshot. I loved stories in which someone small triumphed over a big bully.

As we were leaving the religion class I heard one of my classmates say, "I'd like to make a slingshot and try it out."

This was exactly what I was thinking myself. I

turned to look and saw that the speaker was a plump girl, a little shorter than I was.

"I'm Zhang Xueyan," she said, introducing her- self. "I hear you're a new girl this year."

"Yes," I said. "My name is Tao Ailin. I'm nine years old."

"Hey, we're the same age!" said Xueyan. There was a brightness in her voice and a boldness in her eye that immediately appealed to me. That was how Zhang Xueyan became my closest friend in school.

Since the fees of the MacIntosh School were high, my classmates were all girls from well-to-do families. Most of the girls had bound feet, but three did not. The families of these three girls believed, as Father did, that times were changing in China and that foot binding was cruel and should be abolished. Xueyan was one of the three girls with unbound feet, and what I liked best about her was the fact that she was not ashamed of her big feet. She was proud of them.

"My fiancé's family broke our engagement because of my feet," I confessed to Xueyan. "My mother is afraid nobody will marry me now."

Xueyan laughed. Her laughter was so loud that several of the girls walking ahead of us in the hallway turned and stared. "What's so bad about that?" demanded Xueyan. "I don't intend to get married at all. After finishing this school I'm going to study medicine and become a doctor. Then I won't need a husband to support me."

I admired Xueyan. I copied the way she walked with big, confident steps, and I even tried to talk like her.

In our English-language class, however, I was the leader. I could repeat almost perfectly the sounds made by Miss Gilbertson. For years I had infuriated my relatives by the accurate way I imitated the way they talked. Now it turned out that my gift for mimicry was considered a talent.

"Excellent!" said Miss Gilbertson when it was my turn to recite. "You have a superb ear. You can even go to a college and study to become a teacher of English!"

I was thrilled at the idea, and I began to feel that there was hope for me after all. I didn't have to become a nun, for I could go on to a more advanced school and study to become a teacher. "Can women become teachers, too?"

Miss Gilbertson laughed, and I blushed. *She* was a teacher, and a woman. But of course she was a foreigner, so she was different. "What I mean is, can a *Chinese* woman become a teacher?" I asked.

Miss Gilbertson's face became serious. "I don't personally know of any Chinese women teaching, but I hear there are a few in one of the schools in Shanghai. Things are changing in China. Who knows? By the time you grow up, there may be a lot of Chinese women teachers."

Miss Gilbertson's approval meant a lot to me. I could tell she loved her job, and having a student do well seemed to please her more than anything else

in the world. It would be wonderful to become a
teacher like Miss Gilbertson.

For three years school life occupied most of my
days and most of my thoughts. At home things had
changed. Father spent less time with us, for his
work was very demanding. He was thinner and
seemed tired. Grandmother looked anxiously at
him and kept coaxing him to eat more. Often he
was too tired to join us when we went to eat dinner
with Grandmother. She would complain that everyone was deserting her.

It was true that there were fewer people at her
table those days, since both Eldest Sister and Second Sister had gotten married and left home.

Before Second Sister left, we had a long private
talk. Second Sister began to talk about silkworms,
of all things. "Remember the time when I showed
you a cocoon that was pale green?" she asked.

I remembered the occasion clearly because it was
on the same day that I saw Second Sister washing
her feet. "Yes," I said, "you liked the colored ones
and wished you had more of them."

"I personally like the colored cocoons," said Second Sister, "but silk weavers hate them because
they spoil the white uniformity. Whenever they see
a colored one, they immediately take it out and
burn it. Remember this."

I didn't know what she meant by this reference
to silkworms. Nor did I understand why she often
looked sad in the days just before her wedding.

I asked Grandmother why Second Sister should

be unhappy about getting married. She didn't want to tell me at first but eventually confessed that she had the impression Mrs. Chen, Second Sister's future mother-in-law, was cold and harsh.

Only after Second Sister had left for her husband's home did I finally understand the significance of her remarks about silkworms. Second Sister was warning me about the danger of being different from everyone else. I wasn't sure whether she was talking about *my* danger or her own in the Chen family, where her mother-in-law would come down severely on anyone who dared to show spirit.

I had been close to Second Sister and missed her company, but Little Brother was growing bigger, and I loved playing with him. He made the funniest gurgles when I chased him around our courtyard. The two of us would talk in a mixture of Chinese and English, until his amah stepped in and stopped it.

My brother had a different amah from my old one, who had been sent away when I started school. Maybe she was too dainty and frail to look after a robust little boy. She probably got a new job looking after a nice, quiet little girl with bound feet.

The troubling thing at home was Grandmother's declining health. Grandfather had died when I was in my second year at the school, but he had been in ill health for years, and even when robust he spent most of his time secluded in his study. His death had caused little change in our lives.

Grandmother's illness, however, was different. I

still visited her as much as possible, but she was no longer her usual crusty self after a stroke had left her paralyzed on one side of her body. It wrenched my heart to see her becoming less active and growing steadily weaker.

CHAPTER
FIVE

One morning, during my second year at the MacIntosh School, I was called to the school office and told to return home immediately. Grandmother had had another stroke and was dying.

By the time I reached Grandmother's room, she was unconscious. Listening to her gasping for breath, I remembered her wheezy laughter and her pretended anger every time one of my pranks was reported.

"Come on, we have to leave," said the soft voice of Second Sister. "Other visitors are waiting to come in."

I had seen very little of Second Sister since her marriage and had forgotten how comforting her arms felt around my shoulders. My teachers in school were nice when I did something they approved of. But Grandmother and Second Sister loved me no matter what I did.

The next morning, just before dawn, I woke up to the sound of loud wailing. My sisters and I quickly dressed ourselves in the coarse white hemp robes that had been prepared for us. We ate a hurried breakfast and joined the other mourners for the funeral.

I stood with the rest of the Tao family and added my voice to the wailing. There were so many mourners for Grandmother that our family didn't have to hire professional criers. Besides the Taos, there were people from Grandmother's side of the family. This was a bigger gathering than the one for Grandfather's funeral. Relatives, friends, and servants had truly loved Grandmother.

The days of mourning were so busy that I barely had time to feel sorrow. Guests had to be entertained, and I was called to help serve the refreshments. Even Little Brother passed dishes of candy around. Suddenly I found myself handing a cup of tea to Mrs. Liu—who was no longer my future mother-in-law.

Mrs. Liu bent her head to wipe her eyes. "I know you're sad," she said in a muffled voice. "You loved your grandmother very much."

I tried my best to hold my head with dignity. In the past few hours I had learned a lot about dignity from watching my parents and sisters. "Yes, but you were very fond of Grandmother, too, Mrs. Liu."

"You're right, our families were very close," Mrs. Liu murmured. She looked up at me, and after a moment she sighed. "I want to tell you that our decision about breaking your engagement was a very hard one. We agonized over it for many months. I'm truly sorry, Ailin."

I was glad to go back to school after the mourning period was over. Big Uncle was the official head of the family after the death of Grandfather, but it had been Grandmother who really gave the orders in family matters. Now there seemed to be nobody in charge. Big Uncle's first wife was the one who should be running things, but she was a thin, frightened woman who didn't dare to scold her own sons. Unlike Father, Big Uncle had married a second wife, a more forceful-looking woman. But she was also used to obeying Grandmother's orders and now looked quite lost. Big Uncle himself, of course, couldn't run the household. That was a woman's work. The result was confusion, and that made Big Uncle angry at everybody all the time.

Big Uncle came to eat dinner with us almost every night. In addition to complaining about his wives, he complained about the outside world. A lot of the talk was about who really controlled the country after the Revolution and the fall of the Manchu dynasty.

"I admit the fighting in Hunan and Hubei hasn't spread to our region," Big Uncle said. "But up in the north some of the warlords are getting ready to carve up the country."

Father looked less worried. "The provisional government set up by Sun Yat-sen here in Nanjing seems stable enough. He certainly shows no sign of wanting to make himself emperor."

"It might make our country stronger if he did," grumbled Big Uncle. "Besides, the foreigners will want to take advantage of our weakness to grab whatever they can." He glowered at me for a moment and turned back to Father. "What were you thinking of when you sent this girl to a foreign school? They'll fill her head with strange ideas. As if she didn't have enough of them to start with!"

"Since Ailin isn't marrying the Liu boy, we thought she should study to become a teacher," Mother said.

Big Uncle's face turned red with outrage. I didn't know which made him angrier: Mother's daring to break into a serious conversation about the outside world or the idea of my studying to become a teacher. "A girl, working at an outside job?" he sputtered.

Father coughed. "Don't worry, Elder Brother. It's too soon to think about Ailin's future. Besides, we don't know what our country will be like in ten years' time." After he finished talking he coughed again. In fact, he coughed for quite a while, then took out a handkerchief to wipe his lips.

Big Uncle continued to mutter angrily. "You

keep talking about changes. Nature never changes! Do you really expect men to change into women and grow breasts? Or women to sprout beards? You're—" He broke off and stared at the stained handkerchief in Father's hands.

"I'm all right," Father said, but not before I had seen that there was blood on the cloth.

My heart lurched. Did this mean that Father was suffering from tuberculosis, the dreaded lung disease that had killed my aunt? Was that why he had been looking so thin and tired lately?

In the months that followed, the only thing that took my mind off Father's cough was school. I threw myself frantically into my studies. English was my best subject by far, and Miss Gilbertson praised my pronunciation. As she did with her other advanced students, she gave me a foreign name. She chose Eileen, which I liked very much, since it sounded almost the same as my Chinese name, Ailin. My friend Xueyan also had an English name: Sheila. But she didn't like it very much, and she refused to use it.

With the new name I felt that I had acquired a second personality. At school I was Eileen, speaking English and learning about galaxies and faraway countries such as Russia. At home I was Ailin, a naughty girl whose engagement had been broken.

Soon Miss Gilbertson was asking me to help correct the pronunciation of the other students. "You sound almost exactly like Miss Gilbertson," said

Xueyan. "How do you manage to make those strange sounds so perfectly?"

Not all the students were as nice as Xueyan. Some of them didn't like having me correct their pronunciation, and those with bound feet resented me the most. "She's no better than a peasant girl!" I heard one of them whisper. "Maybe she thinks she can transform herself into a foreigner! She can put some clay on her nose to make it bigger and dye her hair a bright red."

The world history class was taught by Miss Scott, a gaunt woman with frizzy yellow hair. I didn't like her as much as Miss Gilbertson because she enjoyed correcting students when they were wrong and spent less time praising students when they were right. But I was fascinated by her stories about warriors who lived in olden times and were called knights. The pictures in our textbook showed the knights wearing armor that looked as though it were made out of tin cans. Once, our school served an English afternoon meal with dark tea, pastries, and thick milk that came out of a can. Tin cans were a great novelty to us, and I couldn't imagine actually wearing them, much less fighting in a suit made of them.

I was less happy when Miss Scott came to the history of China. She related how one dynasty after another had fallen because of corruption, including the recent Qing (Manchu) Dynasty. Although Father and Big Uncle often talked about the corruption of the court, it made me angry to hear a foreigner criticizing the former rulers of my country.

A year earlier I would have spoken out, but now I knew that contradicting a teacher could bring a severe reprimand from the school. It might even get me expelled.

I had learned caution from what had happened to Xueyan. When Miss Scott said that throughout Chinese history women were no better than slaves, Xueyan raised her hand. "There was a famous woman warrior called Hua Mulan," she said triumphantly. "And the Dowager Empress Wu Zetian of the Tang dynasty actually proclaimed herself a ruling empress and tried to start a new dynasty!"

Even Xueyan, however, did not dare to mention the late Dowager Empress Cixi, whose name still chilled the blood even after her death. I noticed that whenever my parents mentioned the evil and powerful Cixi, their voices were hushed, even after the Revolution had gotten rid of the Manchu Dynasty.

Miss Scott was furious at Xueyan for openly contradicting her and sent her to the principal's office. Xueyan was severely reprimanded, and she was allowed to stay in the school only because her family was wealthy and influential.

It was different for me. Our family, the Taos, had been wealthy for generations. When my sisters got married, box after box of rich gifts had been sent to their husbands' families. That gave my sisters standing with their new in-laws. I hadn't paid much attention to the subject of money until one evening when Big Uncle came to dinner and complained about needless expenses. "With the countryside plagued by soldiers-turned-bandits, we're not getting our rents from our farmers," he said. "We'll have to start cutting down." He glanced at me for a moment and added, "The tuition for the public school is a heavy expense."

Big Uncle would have liked to use any excuse to take me out of school. It was only Father's strong support that prevented Big Uncle from doing what he wanted. "As long as I have my job at the customs office, I can still afford to send Ailin to the school," Father said quietly.

But Father was a sick man. He was coughing a lot now, and his cheeks often had a hectic flush.

School was dismissed early one Friday afternoon, something to do with the Christian religious holiday called Easter. My friends and I had to wait in front of the gate for our rickshaws to come and take us home.

"So it's true!" said a voice. "I heard you were going to a public school, too."

I turned around and saw a boy who looked faintly familiar. The high, raised eyebrows reminded me of someone. "Don't you remember me?" he asked, opening and shutting his mouth a few times.

Of course. This was Liu Hanwei, my former fi-

不
要
纏
足

ancé. My relatives wouldn't let me forget that by refusing to have my feet bound, I had ruined my chance to marry this son of the Liu family.

The last time I had seen him was during our boating expedition on Lake Xuanwu. Now three years older, he was much taller, and his voice had changed. The deeper voice made him seem more mature.

"Hello, Hanwei," I said easily. I indicated Xueyan. "This is my friend, Zhang Xueyan. She and I go to the same school."

Hanwei smiled. "So this is your school, Ailin? How do you like it?"

"It's been really exciting," I said. "Ever since I heard you say that you were going to a public school, I've wanted to go, too."

"My school is just down the street over there," said Hanwei, pointing. "Since we're so close, we might run into each other again." He was about to say more, but then his expression changed. "I'm afraid I have to go now." He turned and walked away quickly to join some older boys who were calling him.

Xueyan looked at him curiously. "Who was that? He seemed interested in you."

"He'd better not be," I said, trying to sound casual. I couldn't help feeling a tiny spurt of pleasure. "We used to be engaged, but his family broke off the engagement when I refused to have my feet bound."

"You haven't really lost much if Hanwei meekly

66

follows his parents' orders," said Xueyan. "It was his mother who decided to break the engagement, wasn't it?"

I hadn't thought much about who had made the decision, but when I remembered Mrs. Liu's expression at Grandmother's funeral, I decided Xueyan was right. Hanwei seemed still interested in me, and it was Mrs. Liu who had decreed that big feet were unacceptable. In the Tao family it had been Grandmother who made the major decisions about marriages and engagements.

"Chinese women have always had a lot of power, in spite of what Miss Scott said," muttered Xueyan.

There was something I could not understand. "If we women are so powerful, why do we submit to the torture of having our feet bound? *Men* don't have to have bound feet!"

Xueyan shook her head. "We do it because our mothers and grandmothers insist on having it done."

I remembered that it had been Mother and Grandmother who had tried to have my feet bound. It had been Father who had finally ordered that the attempts stop. "But I thought it's to please the *men* that women's feet are bound!" I thought back to the teacher of our family school, who had spent so much time on the classics. "According to Master Confucius, women should be submissive to men. Having bound feet certainly made us helpless and therefore submissive."

"In Master Confucius's time, women's feet were

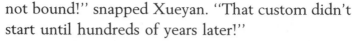

not bound!" snapped Xueyan. "That custom didn't start until hundreds of years later!"

Since Xueyan was the expert on history, I didn't try to argue with her. "Why do mothers keep forcing this gruesome practice on their daughters?" I asked.

"Maybe they want their daughters to experience the same pain they themselves had to endure," said Xueyan.

I found it hard to believe that my mother was as cruel as that. But it was still a mystery to me why a boy's mother would interfere when he himself was willing to accept a girl with big feet. I could tell that Hanwei was still interested in me. The strange thing was that at Grandmother's funeral, even Mrs. Liu had seemed sorry to break our engagement. Then why had she done it? Because of tradition?

My classmates who had bound feet did their best to make me feel like a social outcast. But who had decided that big feet were unacceptable in the first place? It wasn't Master Confucius, according to Xueyan.

Generations of girls had to suffer excruciating pain because somebody unknown had decreed that big feet were unacceptable in upper-class society. It was high time that somebody tried to stop this senseless practice. I was proud that Xueyan and I were among the first to rebel.

CHAPTER
SIX

Father's illness was something I had tried to push
to the back of my mind. I knew he hadn't been
going to work, and I tried to convince myself that it
was because not all the government bureaucracies
had been running smoothly. But it was getting
harder to ignore the telltale signs of Father's lung
disease: the fits of coughing, which ended with
blood on his handkerchiefs.

He still found time to talk to me, however. He
was very curious about my experiences at school,
especially about my world history class. "It's not
too late for our country if more young people can
learn about the outside world," he remarked as we
sat in his study.

I told him about Xueyan's argument with Miss
Scott. Father laughed so hard that he started coughing again. When he could speak again his face was

sober. "It's been seven years since the Revolution. We still have some problems with the transition from the imperial government to the republic. We have to learn how other countries have dealt with this transition."

I was very proud that he was talking things over with me as if I were an adult. But I was tiring him out. Mother came in with a cup of hot ginger tea. "You'd better drink this and get some rest," she said to Father.

One winter afternoon five months later, I found Second Sister in my room when I returned home. I was so happy to see her that I didn't notice anything wrong at first. Then I saw the expression on her face. "What's the matter, Second Sister?" I asked.

"Ailin, do you know how sick Father is?" she asked.

"I know he hasn't been going to work," I said. "I thought it was because government bureaucracies, like the customs office, aren't yet back to normal after the Revolution."

Second Sister's mouth fell open. "He talks to you about government bureacracies?"

"Well, I also listen to Father and Big Uncle while they're talking to each other at dinner," I admitted.

"I guess I didn't pay attention to the men's conversation," said Second Sister. "I didn't think it was any concern of mine."

If that comment had came from Mother, I would have interpreted it as criticism. But on Second Sister's face I saw regret. "I've always been nosy," I mumbled. "Everybody keeps saying so."

Second Sister ran her hand absently over the satin coverlet on my bed. After a moment she broke the silence. "I'm visiting because Father is very sick, Ailin."

I had to swallow hard before I could speak. "Yes, I know."

Second Sister's voice was shaky. "Ailin, you'll have to think about what you will do when Father . . . when Father is no longer here to support you."

Suddenly I felt cold, and I wrapped my arms tightly around myself. "You mean I can't continue school and study to become a teacher?"

"It was Father who made the decision to send you to school," said Second Sister. "When he is no longer here to pay the tuition, I'm afraid you'll have to drop out of school."

I had not forgotten what Big Uncle had said about the decline of the family income from our tenant farmers. Even if we had been as rich as we had been formerly, I knew that Big Uncle would have stopped my schooling if the decision had been his to make. And when Father was gone, Big Uncle would be making all the decisions about my future.

Father died five weeks later. The funeral rites were not as elaborate as those for Grandmother, and I felt a burning resentment as I stood weeping loudly

不
要
纏
足

with my sisters and the other women. Big Uncle had spent lavishly for Grandmother's funeral but much less on Father's. According to tradition, of course, it was normal for a man to pay more attention to his mother's funeral, but this didn't make me less angry.

I stared at Big Uncle with hatred, condemning him for his stinginess. His face looked more deeply lined, and his shoulders, usually squared in self-righteousness or hunched in anger, had an unfamiliar droop. Suddenly I realized that Big Uncle was grieving as much as I was. I disliked him for many reasons, but I was forced to admit that he had loved Father deeply.

When the mourning period ended, my sisters returned home to their husbands, and I took off my white mourning robe. That very afternoon I was summoned to Big Uncle's rooms.

Big Uncle's two wives were in the reception room. They spoke to me in soft, kind voices, but they did not meet my eyes. After they had served tea and put out some candied peanuts, they quickly retreated to an inner room.

Big Uncle wasted no time. "You will not be returning to school," he said.

My heart was beating fast, but I tried to hide my fear. "Why not?" I asked.

"Because I say so!" snapped Big Uncle.

I managed to make my lips smile. "I used to say that!" After a moment I added, "When I was much younger, of course."

Big Uncle's eyes bulged, but otherwise he kept his face impassive. "Since you always eavesdrop on adult conversations, you must know that we have to cut down on unnecessary expenses. The tuition for your school is an unnecessary expense."

"The tuition has already been paid for this term," I said. "Therefore it would be a waste of money for me to stop school. You said yourself that we should not be wasteful."

"This insolence is the result of your going to a foreign school!" cried Big Uncle.

I blinked hard to prevent my tears from falling. "Father wanted me to go to this school. He died only a week ago. Are you planning to go against his wishes already?"

Big Uncle no longer tried to hide his fury. "Do you know that I am the head of the Tao family and that I have the right to order you to be strangled and your body thrown down a well?"

I felt I was choking, and my legs threatened to buckle under me. "No, under our new government you don't have that right any longer. It is now illegal for you to put a family member to death. If you do, you will be arrested as a criminal."

Big Uncle's face turned a dark red, and for a moment I was certain he was going to raise his hand and strike me. That was still legal under the new laws.

As Big Uncle struggled for breath, I heard a rustle behind me. Big Uncle's first wife beckoned. "You'd better come into my room and sit with me for a while. It's not safe for you when he's like that."

I knew she was right. Following her, I thought this was the bravest thing this slender, browbeaten woman had ever done.

Big Uncle did not try to stop me from returning to school for the remaining two months of the term. I counted each precious day, determined to make the most of the time left to me. I studied as I had never done before.

I told Xueyan about the situation at home, and she spread the news to the other students. Soon even the teachers heard about my uncle's decision to discontinue my schooling.

Miss Gilbertson spoke to me after the classes were over one day. "Eileen, you're the best student I've ever had in my English class. You have a very good ear, and your pronunciation is almost perfect. All you need is a bigger vocabulary. I know you won't be able to return to school next year, but I'm willing to give you free tutoring at my home. I can't bear to see this talent for languages being wasted."

At Miss Gilbertson's kindness I broke down and wept, something I hadn't done under Big Uncle's attacks. It was not the easy, melodious wailing I had participated in at funerals, but a painful sobbing that scraped my throat. Finally I hiccuped to a stop and tried to wipe my streaming face with the sleeve of my blue cotton coverall.

"Here, use this," said Miss Gilbertson gruffly, offering me a handkerchief. When I finished wiping my face and tried to return the sodden ball of linen,

Miss Gilbertson smiled and shook her head. "You can keep the handkerchief, Eileen."

The handkerchief, embroidered with the name *Frances Gilbertson*, remains among my most precious belongings to this day.

Not all the teachers were as sympathetic as Miss Gilbertson. I think Miss Scott regarded me and Xueyan as her two troublemakers. She sounded almost glad that at least one of them was not returning. "Well, you must do whatever your guardian wishes," she said to me, pursing her lips. "He must have your future all planned."

Big Uncle's plans for my future worried me more than anything else. It was impossible to guess what he had in mind, since he seemed to avoid me at home as much as I avoided him. I tried to get information from Mother, but every time I brought up the subject of Big Uncle's intentions, her eyes would fill with tears.

As the term approached its end, the girls who were graduating began making sentimental farewells. Some of them coyly hinted that marriages were being arranged for them by their families.

I felt a pang every time marriage plans were mentioned. "Don't pay any attention to them," said Xueyan. "Those girls are empty-headed fools who think their whole world begins and ends with getting a husband."

"It's not envy I feel," I said. "It's fear. I have no idea what sort of husband my uncle has in mind for me."

不
要
纏
足

Xueyan gave me a sidelong glance. "What about that boy we saw last year, the one who used to be your fiancé? What was his name again?"

"Liu Hanwei," I muttered. "I don't think about him anymore. He's out of my life."

"Well, I don't plan to get married at all!" declared Xueyan. "I plan to be a doctor and support myself with my own earnings."

Looking at my friend's determined face, I decided that Xueyan might be able to do just that. Of course, her family had already promised that they would pay for medical school once Xueyan graduated from MacIntosh.

As for my hope of becoming an English teacher, it looked like an impossible dream. In one more week I would be finished with schooling for the rest of my life.

On the last day of school there was a general assembly at which good-byes were said for the year, or forever. Listening to the speeches by the outstanding students of the graduating class, I realized that I would never be one of these girls onstage, looking tearful, joyous, and proud.

What saved the day for me was a whispered message from Miss Gilbertson. "Don't forget, Eileen: Beginning next week, I'll expect you at my house for tutoring."

The end of the school year was the beginning of the hot, humid summer. Nanjing, called one of the Three Ovens of China, became a city of hazy lethargy. Even the beggars were quiet as they languidly held out their begging bowls to passersby.

At home nobody seemed to notice when I slipped out the front gate early each morning and rode away in a rickshaw sent by Miss Gilbertson. I had told Mother about the tutoring. She shook her head hopelessly but made no objections. At least she was reassured by the rickshaw. Her daughter wouldn't have to walk through the streets like a servant girl, an entertainer, or a peasant.

I wasn't sure whether Big Uncle knew of the tutoring. He probably suspected, but he did nothing to stop it.

At the beginning of the first tutoring session, I tried to express my gratitude toward Miss Gilbertson. "Someday I'll find a way to repay you!"

"I'm doing this for my own satisfaction, so we'll skip all this politeness," Miss Gilbertson said briskly. "I don't have time to waste, and neither do you."

She got down to business and opened her book. I found myself working harder than I had ever done before. There were no slower students to hold us back, and as soon as I had mastered one section, Miss Gilbertson moved on quickly to the next one.

The heat was terrible. One day I saw perspiration dripping down Miss Gilbertson's nose and splashing onto the desk. I laughed when I realized that the same thing was happening with me. We were both intoxicated: she by the joy of teaching and I by the joy of learning.

不
要
纏
足

After a few weeks Miss Gilbertson and I began speaking entirely in English. One day our lesson was interrupted by voices in the hall. I heard someone saying in English, "I didn't know Frances was taking on private pupils."

Miss Gilbertson looked up. "I'm afraid we'll have to stop for the day, Eileen. An old friend of mine has come to visit."

She got up quickly and went to the door. "Imogene! Come in! Let me introduce my prize pupil from the MacIntosh School."

A tall, blond woman came into the room. I rose and shook hands with the newcomer, as I had been taught. "This is Eileen Tao," said Miss Gilbertson. "And this is Imogene Warner. The Warners are old friends who have just arrived in Nanjing from Shanghai."

This was how I first met a member of the Warner family. I learned later from Miss Gilbertson that Mr. and Mrs. Warner were both missionaries, and that they had lived in Shanghai for almost six years before being transferred to Nanjing. They had two children. Grace was six years old. Billy, who was five, had been born in China. Like other missionaries, however, they had "furloughs," time off from work, when they could go back to their homes. The Warners' home was in San Francisco, a large city on the West Coast of the United States.

All these things I learned and stored away in my memory, although at the time I didn't know how important they would be to me.

CHAPTER
SEVEN

Big Uncle made his move on an evening in late summer, when the first cool breezes began to blow through the courtyards. I sat outside with Mother and Little Brother. I was trying to teach him an English song about some mice who were blind. The maids were giggling, and even Mother wore a happy smile. Little Brother laughed so hard that he slipped from his stool and lay on his back, waving his legs in the air.

Suddenly the maids became silent, and I saw Mother's smile fade. One of Big Uncle's maids was coming through the round moon gate. "Miss Three, the master would like to see you."

"I'll come with you, Ailin," said Mother, her voice trembling.

"The master said Miss Three is to come alone," said the maid.

不
要
纏
足

I looked at the expression on Mother's face. "Has he made a decision about my future?"

Mother put her arms around me. "He has been approached by a matchmaker." She swallowed hard. "Since your father's death, Ailin, Big Uncle is the one who will be deciding your future. Please don't make him angry."

The maid coughed. "The master is waiting."

I pulled myself gently from Mother's arms. "I'd better go before Big Uncle gets even angrier with me."

Big Uncle was seated in his front room, sipping a cup of tea. He motioned me to a stool opposite him. As usual, he did not waste time in coming to the point. "We cannot support indefinitely a female who contributes nothing to the family."

I wanted to point out that if he had allowed me to continue school, I could have become a teacher and contributed my salary to the family. But I knew it would be useless.

"As you know," continued Big Uncle, "the Lius have broken off your engagement to Hanwei."

I certainly didn't need a reminder of that fact, since it had been a recurring topic in my family. Besides, it had happened years before. "Mother said you had heard from a matchmaker," I said.

"If you will stop interrupting, I can explain." Big Uncle took a sip of tea and studied the pattern of his eggshell porcelain cup. Suddenly I realized he was uncomfortable. That only increased my foreboding.

Big Uncle cleared his throat. "The second son in the Feng family wants another woman for his chamber. He already has two wives, but they've produced only girls, and the family isn't ready to contract for another wife. Therefore, they decided on a concubine for him."

I felt hot blood rush into my face. A concubine was little better than a slave, since she was brought into the household without any contract or exchange of gifts between her family and the man's family. She did not have the rights or standing of a wife, even a secondary wife. "If you do this to me, you will disgrace the whole Tao family!"

"You're the last person to talk about disgracing the Tao family!" cried Big Uncle. "By refusing to have your feet bound, you've made it impossible for us to arrange a decent marriage for you!"

"There are other things I can do! I don't have to descend to being a concubine!"

"What, for instance?" demanded Big Uncle. "Are you thinking of marrying a farmer? Farm women can have big feet, since they toil in the fields. Some of our tenant farmers could use a hard-working wife."

I suddenly remembered my amah. I hadn't thought of that pathetic little woman in years. Now I wondered what had happened to her. "I can become an amah," I declared. "My old amah took the job because her family was too poor to support her."

Big Uncle banged his teacup down so hard that it

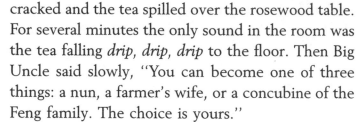

cracked and the tea spilled over the rosewood table. For several minutes the only sound in the room was the tea falling *drip, drip, drip* to the floor. Then Big Uncle said slowly, "You can become one of three things: a nun, a farmer's wife, or a concubine of the Feng family. The choice is yours."

For several days Big Uncle said nothing more about the offer from the Feng family. But I knew better than to relax. Who could protect me? I had no money, not a copper. With Father gone, we had no income other than what Big Uncle saw fit to give us. Mother had some jewelry she could sell, but that would be needed to educate Little Brother.

It was so unfair! Any money we had was used for educating the boys in the family, but money spent on girls was considered wasted. I thought of Big Uncle's sons. After they had finished the family schools, expensive tutors had been hired to continue their education. And what was the result? One son worked as a clerk in the customs office, but he was so sloppy and incompetent that even family connections couldn't get him the promotion he wanted.

My two sisters had no education beyond the family schools, and they faced the closed life of an upper-class wife. Second Sister's status was higher than that of a secondary wife or concubine, but with a cold, harsh mother-in-law, her life would be no happier.

In my case, I had had an unusually indulgent

grandmother and loving father. Some would even say that they had spoiled me—and spoiled me for normal life. Without education, what was left for me to do?

Could my friend Zhang Xueyan do anything to help? Although I hadn't seen Xueyan since the end of the school term, I knew where the Zhangs lived. If Big Uncle tried to do something really outrageous, I could send a message to my friend and make sure the Zhangs knew about it. They were a wealthy and influential family, and their opinion counted.

The trouble was that even if Xueyan's family openly criticized Big Uncle, they could do nothing legally to stop him. Besides, I had no way of knowing whether Xueyan's parents would side with me.

Traditionally the strongest weapon that a Chinese woman had was suicide. Time after time women who had been deeply wronged killed themselves. Even when the wrong had been concealed from outsiders, the angry ghost of the dead woman would haunt the perpetrator. But I refused to consider suicide. I didn't have complete confidence that my angry ghost would come back to haunt Big Uncle.

I was left with one idea: working as an amah and looking after other people's children. When I mentioned the possibility to Mother, however, she sighed. "Ailin, you must be well bred to work as an amah in a decent family. The children are supposed to copy your manners and behavior."

不
要
纏
足

"I *am* well bred! I'm still Miss Tao! Nothing can change that!"

Mother shook her head with a mixture of sadness and amusement. "You show no respect to your elders. You talk too much. Worst of all, Ailin, you have big feet."

"Having big feet disqualifies me as an amah?" I couldn't believe people could be that stupid. "You'd think parents would *want* an amah who could run after the children and catch them. *Mine* was always hobbling after me and whining. That's why I always got away from her!"

"If people hear you talk about running away from your amah," said Mother, "they certainly will not want you to look after their children."

Miss Gilbertson was a friend, but what could she do to help? She was not a relative, and she was a foreigner.

One day, as the summer drew to a close and the opening of school approached, Miss Gilbertson said, "Eileen, I'm afraid we'll have to stop these tutoring sessions soon. Once I go back to teaching, I won't have any free time left."

I tried to answer cheerfully, but my lips were trembling, and for once my English deserted me completely.

"What's the matter?" asked Miss Gilbertson. "I'm not saying good-bye forever! We can still keep in touch."

"No, we can't," I said. Then it all poured out. I told Miss Gilbertson about the three choices given me by Big Uncle: to become a concubine, a nun, or the wife of a tenant farmer. "Of the three, I prefer to marry a farmer and plod around the rice paddies on my big feet. Maybe I can speak English to the water buffalo."

Miss Gilbertson looked shocked. "Are these the only choices open to a respectable young woman?"

"My uncle doesn't think I'm respectable. I thought of becoming an amah, but my mother says upper-class parents prefer to have someone with bound feet."

"Wait, I've just thought of something," said Miss Gilbertson. "You enjoy looking after children?"

"I'm very good with my younger brother," I said proudly. The expression on Miss Gilbertson's face gave me hope. "Do you know of someone who wants an amah? One with big feet?"

"My friends, the Warners, want someone to take care of their two children," Miss Gilbertson said slowly. "They have a Chinese amah at the moment, but the children don't pay any attention to her and are running completely wild. Imogene Warner said she would give anything to have an amah who speaks English."

The name Warner sounded familiar, and then I remembered what Miss Gilbertson had told me about her friends. "I've already met Mrs. Warner, right here, in fact."

Miss Gilbertson smiled. "So you have! I'll send word to Imogene right away and see if we can arrange a meeting."

Apparently the Warners' need was so great that they asked to see me the very next day. Miss Gilbertson took me to a modern, two-story house in a part of town with wide streets. It seemed bizarre for a house to have rooms built directly above other rooms. If you stamped your feet on the second floor, dust might fall into the rice bowls of people eating dinner below you!

As soon as Miss Gilbertson and I were shown in by the houseboy, a very tall, thin foreign man came in. He had sparse brown hair, but to make up for it, he had the bushiest mustache I had ever seen. "This is so good of you, Frances!" he said, shaking hands with Miss Gilbertson. He turned to me. "So you are Eileen. Miss Gilbertson has told us a lot about you."

I held out my hand. "How do you do, Mr. Warner?"

Mr. Warner beamed. "Why, your English is perfect!"

"I've been lucky to have Miss Gilbertson as my teacher," I said. For a moment the three of us stood smiling at one another. The silence was broken by thumps that started above our heads and moved slowly down the curved staircase.

Mrs. Warner appeared first, holding the hands of a girl with a shiny red face and masses of bouncing blond curls. A younger boy followed them. His face was scowling, and his thumping steps told the world that he was ready to rebel against anything and everything.

I instantly recognized a kindred spirit.

"Hello, Eileen," said Mrs. Warner. "I'm very glad to see you again. This is our daughter, Grace, who is six." She turned and tried to propel the boy to the front, but he quickly moved around so that he stayed behind her. "This is our son, Billy. He's five, but sometimes he acts like a two-year-old."

"Do you think you would be able to be our amah?" asked Mr. Warner. I could see desperation in his light blue eyes.

"Timothy," whispered Mrs. Warner to her husband, "Eileen looks a bit young."

"How old are you, my dear?" Mr. Warner asked me.

"I'm fourteen," I said instantly. Miss Gilbertson raised her eyebrows, since she knew I was not quite thirteen. But according to Chinese reckoning, a person is one year old at the moment of birth, and another year is added to everyone's age on New Year's Day. Since I had been born in November, I was counted as two when I was less than three months old. Therefore, I was telling the absolute truth when I said I was fourteen.

"I'm very bad at guessing the ages of the Chinese," confessed Mrs. Warner. "They always look a lot younger than they really are."

"Fourteen is old enough," said Mr. Warner with

relief. He turned to me. "We would be delighted if you would accept the position of amah for Grace and Billy."

"Of course, you will be living with us in the house," said Mrs. Warner. "You can have a large room upstairs all to yourself."

I felt a pang in my chest at the thought of leaving my home, with its courtyards, fragrant sweet-olive bushes, carp pond, and the maids who did my bidding. But I would be leaving that home in any case. My alternatives were to become a concubine of the Fengs, enter a nunnery, or live in a thatched farmhouse with mud walls.

I swallowed hard. "Yes, I would be happy to work here."

CHAPTER
EIGHT

When I went to tell Big Uncle about my decision, I was so nervous that my legs wobbled like meat jelly. I remembered vividly our interview soon after Father's death, when Big Uncle had threatened to have me strangled and thrown down a well. Nor did I forget my defiant answer, which had not been calculated to soothe his anger. Somehow I managed to walk without tottering to his courtyard and into his study. I found him seated behind his table, waiting for me.

"I've decided to go and work as an amah for an American missionary family," I announced baldly. "I will be living with them from now on."

Instead of exploding with fury, Big Uncle looked at me with no expression at all. For a moment I thought he had not heard what I had said. Then he smiled—or more accurately, he bared his teeth. "I had thought that nothing you did would surprise me anymore. It seems I am wrong."

The calmness of his voice emboldened me, and I ventured to explain my decision. "I thought it less disgraceful to the family name than becoming a concubine of the Fengs."

I had made a mistake. What I took for calmness was fury under tight control. His fingers gripped the inkstone on his desk. It was heavy and would make a deadly missile. Then he loosened his hold. It took such an effort that I saw the drops of sweat on his brow. "I loved your father," he said in a strangled voice. "That's why you may leave this room alive."

Mother was the one I told next. As I had expected, she was appalled. "Living with the foreigners is different from just going to their school, Ailin!" she cried. "Can you stand eating all that foreign food? And you might end up wearing their funny clothes, all made of wool and terribly itchy!"

I tried to reassure her. "Don't worry, Mother. I've tried some foreign food at the MacIntosh School, and it didn't disagree with me. As for clothes, I'll be wearing my own."

Saying good-bye to Little Brother was harder. "Why are you going away to take care of somebody else's children?" he asked. "Why can't you stay here with me?"

I looked him in the eye, the way Second Sister used to look at me when she had something serious to say. "Little Brother, all girls have to leave home eventually. Only boys are allowed to stay. Some girls go to a nunnery, but most go away to join other families. It so happens that the family I'm joining consists of foreigners."

Little Brother wiped his eyes. "Can you visit me? Second Sister comes home sometimes."

I wasn't sure how much freedom the Warners would give me to go out. But I did know one thing: When a married daughter returned home for a visit, she was treated like an empress. Nothing was too good for her. I suspected that if *I* returned home, Big Uncle might order that I be turned away at the door.

"I'll try to visit you if I possibly can," I promised.

The actual moving was less painful than saying my farewells. Since Mrs. Warner had told me that there would be bedding and furniture in my room, all I had to take with me were my clothes and a few personal possessions such as books, pens, writing brush, and ink stick and slab. Everything went into one rickshaw, while I rode in another. As my rickshaw pulled away I turned my head to avoid looking back at the gate of my family home.

Mr. and Mrs. Warner were at work when I arrived with my luggage. The houseboy answered the door, and he looked surly when I asked for help in carrying my bags to my room. Instead of replying, he turned his back on me and barked some orders to a maid, who hurried over to help.

I decided to ignore the houseboy's rudeness. My

major concern at the moment was managing the two children who were my charges.

I knew that Billy would be the difficult one, and I had spent some time thinking over ways to cope with him. As it turned out, I made a good start when I began to unpack my belongings. I was placing my writing implements on the desk in my room when I heard a voice. "What are those things?"

I turned around and saw two heads poking around my door. Grace and Billy came into the room. "Mother said we should let you unpack first," said Grace. "But we wanted to talk to you without the grown-ups."

Billy pointed to the ink stick and little stone slab. "What are those things?" he asked again.

"These are for making ink," I replied.

"We've already got ink," said Grace. "Father has a big bottle of it, only we aren't allowed to touch it."

"This ink is for Chinese brush writing," I told them. "You need very thick ink for that." I had an idea. "Grace, can you get me a glass of water? I'll show you how to grind ink and write Chinese characters."

Grace ran off and quickly returned with a cup of water. Pouring a few drops into a depression in the stone slab, I began to rub the ink stick in the little puddle. I let Grace and Billy take turns rubbing the ink stick, having made them solemnly promise to do it slowly and not spill a drop. When a thick pool of ink had formed, I uncapped a brush, dipped it in the ink, and slowly wrote the characters for *moun-tain* and *river*.

"Whenever you're especially good," I promised them, "I'll let you make some ink and write one of these characters."

The children looked at me with wide eyes. From my own experience I knew they must have received plenty of bribes from adults. But never before had they been bribed by being taught to write in Chinese.

My life as an amah was much harder than I had expected. My own amah had been expected only to get me dressed, carry me around, and prevent me from getting into mischief. With the Warners, I discovered that I was supposed to teach the children as well. Mornings were set aside for lessons, including reading and writing.

"When Frances Gilbertson told us what an excellent student you were," Mrs. Warner said to me, "we counted ourselves lucky to have you teaching Grace and Billy!"

Afraid to point out that I had never taught anyone in my life, I meekly accepted the lesson books. Brightly illustrated and with big print, they were very different from the textbooks I had used at the MacIntosh School. At least they were in easy English. To Grace I read the sentences aloud and had her repeat them after me.

To Billy I had to teach the alphabet first, and he was an unruly pupil. He was very different from

Little Brother, although they were the same age. Little Brother was easy to please and easy to amuse. With Billy I had to use all my ingenuity. Recognizing my own rebellious nature in the boy, I tried to imagine how I myself would react. Sometimes this tactic worked.

The best way to quiet Billy down was to tell him stories. I loved stories involving plenty of action, and these were the ones that he liked best, too. So I told him stories from *Outlaws of the Marsh*, a book about a band of 108 outlaws who defied corrupt government officials.

"I like the part about Wu Song killing the tiger!" yelled Billy, who preferred the bloodthirsty bits.

My own favorite stories were from the classic *Journey to the West*, about the Monkey King who escorted the priest Xuan Zang on a pilgrimage to India. The stories were full of magic and demon spirits, and, of course, action. The only trouble was that instead of quieting Billy down, they sometimes got him even more excited.

What I didn't enjoy was being at the beck and call of the children and having to drop whatever I was doing if one of them wanted my attention. I was in no position to say, "Don't bother me with such a trivial thing!" It made me feel guilty to realize how often my own amah must have wanted to say that.

But taking care of the children was the easiest part. I had to adjust to an entirely new way of life. At the Warners', I no longer had anyone to fetch things for me, to run errands. I discovered immediately that the servants would not do my bidding. The houseboy went out of his way to make this clear.

From the day I arrived I could tell that the houseboy resented me. He was a thin man in his forties, and he gave orders to all the Chinese servants. It took me a while to understand the cause of his resentment. Mr. Warner spoke very little Chinese and Mrs. Warner none at all. The houseboy, who understood some English, ran the household and regarded himself as a vital link between the Warners and the servants. He saw my arrival as a threat to his power, and I often found him glaring angrily at me. Whenever I made some social blunder, which happened often during my early days as an amah, I would see him smile with satisfaction.

The hardest part of all was trying to live the life of a foreigner. Three months after moving in with the Warners, I found that I was growing out of my clothes. I didn't know what to do. At home my clothes had always been made to order, but none of the maids at the Warners' was a seamstress.

Mrs. Warner had a suggestion. "We have our clothes made by a tailor in town. Why don't you have some Western clothes made, Eileen?"

"Yes, yes, Eileen!" shouted Grace. "I want to see you wearing American clothes!"

With the money the Warners paid me I ordered two outfits, similar to those worn by Mrs. Warner but of plainer material and with shorter skirts. I was

不要纏足

used to wearing long trousers under a tunic, and it felt funny to be wearing thick stockings under a skirt. The stockings were uncomfortably binding, but they turned out to be warm as the weather became cooler.

Food was another problem. The first meal I had with the Warner family was a Sunday dinner—which was in the middle of the day! All the Warners ate together, and I joined them at the long, rectangular dining table. Before the meal was served, Mr. Warner said grace for the food provided, ending his prayer with the word *Amen.*

To be on the safe side, I said "Amen," too. Both Mr. and Mrs. Warner beamed when they heard me.

After the prayer I finally took a close look at the plate in front of me. It contained some vegetables and a great slab of meat. For a moment I thought I was supposed to slice it up for everyone else. Did my duties include kitchen work as well? But why do it at the dining table?

"Don't you like beef, Eileen?" asked Mrs. Warner when I didn't pick up my eating utensils right away.

"Yes, yes, I do," I said, although I preferred pork to beef. Hurriedly I picked up my knife and fork, which I had learned to use at the MacIntosh School. I looked around and saw that there was a slab of meat on every plate, although the ones on the children's plates were smaller. Mrs. Warner took her knife and proceeded to cut up the meat on Billy's plate. I realized that *each person* was supposed to eat a whole thick piece! It took all my willpower to finish the serving on my plate. Fortunately only Sunday dinner featured large portions of meat. Most of the other meals consisted of Chinese food, which I was glad to discover the Warners enjoyed.

Usually I ate with the children in an upstairs room. The first time Grace told me that I would be eating with her and Billy, I decided I would enjoy the informality. Then I overheard a conversation between the houseboy and one of the maids.

I was sitting at a small table with Grace and Billy when I heard the houseboy talking to the maid in the hallway. "Why shouldn't she eat with the children?" he said. "She's just hired help. And another thing, I heard you calling her Miss Tao. There's no need for that."

"But she's well bred," protested the maid. "I don't feel right, treating her like one of us."

The houseboy and the maid had not bothered to lower their voices. They had become accustomed to speaking freely in Chinese, secure in the knowledge that the Warner family could not understand.

"What's the matter, Eileen?" asked Grace, who noticed my mortification. "Don't you like to be here with us?"

"Of course I do," I said quickly, but my face was hot, and I felt a mixture of emotions. No one had called me well bred for a long time, not since I had refused to have my feet bound. But it hurt to know that I was now considered by the servants to be one of *them*. Was this how my own amah had felt the first time she went to work?

The servants were not the only ones who didn't bother to lower their voices. Mr. and Mrs. Warner were used to being surrounded by people who didn't understand English.

"I saw Eileen teaching Grace and Billy to write with a brush," Mrs. Warner said one evening after the children were in bed. They were in the living room downstairs, but their voices carried upstairs, and I could hear every word, since my door was open.

"I don't see anything wrong with that," said Mr. Warner.

"Timothy, I don't want the children to learn a heathen language," said Mrs. Warner. "She can spend the time teaching Billy to read and write *English* words."

I got up quietly and closed my door. I didn't want to hear any more. What was wrong with teaching the children to use a brush? They loved it, especially Billy, and he was behaving better in order to earn the privilege of using the brush.

In my history class at the MacIntosh School, Miss Scott had used the word *heathen* to describe various "uncivilized" tribes who practiced strange religions. What did this have to do with Chinese writing?

A few weeks later I heard the word *heathen* again. I knew that on the day called Sunday by the foreigners, all the Warners went out for a "service."

I didn't know what they served, but they were always well dressed. After they came back, the whole family, including me, would eat Sunday dinner together.

One Sunday Mr. Warner asked me to speak with him privately after the meal. I joined him in the room he called the library. It had shelves filled with smelly books bound in leather. The thought of books being bound with the skins of animals revolted me at first, but I had to admit that I was getting used to my new shoes, which were made of pigskin.

I was nervous. Was Mr. Warner planning to send me away because I was two years younger than he had thought? Or because I was teaching Grace and Billy brush writing?

Mr. Warner motioned me to a seat opposite him. He folded his hands and looked at me seriously. "Eileen, you have been very good with the children. They are better behaved, and they seem to be studying well, too."

I knew that tone of voice. Mr. Warner was about to criticize me for something. On the previous day Billy had been jumping from his bed to the floor while I was telling him the story of the Monkey King flying through the air. Mr. and Mrs. Warner had been away at the time, but the houseboy could have reported the thumping.

Mr. Warner continued. "We appreciate your telling Grace and Billy some Chinese folktales. Mrs. Warner and I feel, however, that the time would be better spent on Western history and literature, materials more relevant to our children's own background."

"I thought Grace and Billy would enjoy hearing a different kind of story," I said. "I love stories about foreign countries, myself."

Mr. Warner frowned. "Please let me go on. Folktales are harmless enough. What concerned us more was that you were also discussing Confucianism."

I had mentioned Confucius when the children asked me about my own schooling. I had described the classical works I had studied at my family school. "Master Confucius believed that rulers should be chosen by their virtue, not by their birth or station," I had told Grace and Billy.

I didn't see what Mr. Warner found objectionable. "Why shouldn't the children hear about Confucianism?" I asked.

"Confucianism is a *heathen* religion!" said Mr. Warner. His pale eyes were intent. "I don't want Grace and Billy—"

"Confucianism isn't a religion," I said. "My teacher said it is really a philosophy."

"Don't interrupt me," snapped Mr. Warner. "Confucianism involves idolatry. . . ."

He went on for some time. After a while I stopped listening to him. I felt sick. There was something familiar about Mr. Warner's tone of voice, except that I had last heard it from someone speaking Chinese: Big Uncle. Neither man would tolerate being interrupted by an impertinent slip of a girl.

After Mr. Warner stopped, I nodded meekly and went upstairs to my room. I took down my dictionary and looked up *idolatry*. Reading the definition made my head swell with indignation. I had grown up learning about the wisdom of Master Confucius, who believed that a country should be ruled by benevolence, not force. That constituted idolatry?

Grandfather had often said he was a Confucianist, and he was one of the most scholarly men I had ever known. But in Mr. Warner's opinion, he had been a blind worshiper of something barbaric and unenlightened.

For the first time I understood the price I was paying for my rebellion. I had been exiled from my own people, and I had entered a world that despised what I had been taught to value.

CHAPTER
NINE

During my next two years with the Warners, I lived wholly as Eileen, and only rarely did the girl known as Ailin emerge. Miss Gilbertson was my only link with my past. She came to visit the Warners occasionally, and once, she even invited me to a party she was giving for her students. Xueyan was at the party, and meeting her and my former classmates was a bittersweet experience, with the bitter outweighing the sweet. Xueyan and I held hands but found it hard to speak to each other. I never went to another of Miss Gilbertson's parties.

My family I didn't see at all. During the first New Year's Day with the Warners, I almost made up my mind to visit my home. New Year was always a rollicking time for young people, a time when we bowed to our elder relatives, received gifts of money from them, and gorged ourselves on seasonal treats.

But the two elder relatives I loved best were gone, and I couldn't face the pain of being turned away at the door on Big Uncle's orders. I stayed away from the Tao family residence.

After half a year, Mr. and Mrs. Warner seemed to have gotten over their fear of harboring a heathen idol-worshiper under their roof. At Sunday dinners, after the grace, I always made a point of saying "Amen," and this helped to reassure them.

I stopped talking to Grace and Billy about Confucius, although I still told them some of the more exciting Chinese stories I knew—when I was sure their parents were not listening.

By the time I had been with them for a year, the Warners showed clearly that they were happy about the way I managed the children. When Miss Gilbertson came to call on the Warners, they never failed to thank her for recommending me to them.

More than once Mrs. Warner said to me, "I don't know how you do it, Eileen, but Billy is much better these days."

He had been very difficult after their move to Nanjing. He had left all his friends behind in Shanghai, and boredom and loneliness had driven him into mischief. One of the maids told me, for instance, that Billy would catch cockroaches and put them in the rice pot, but she was afraid to report him to Mr. or Mrs. Warner. I had to stifle a laugh when I heard that, since I still remembered putting earthworms in my amah's bowl of noodles.

I worked hard at keeping the children busy and interested, so Billy had less time to think up tricks. The servants were grateful to me for making their life easier. The only person still hostile was the houseboy.

After almost two years without major mishaps, I must have earned the trust of Mr. and Mrs. Warner. They proved this one day.

"We are going to be away for two nights, Eileen," Mrs. Warner said. Her tone was cheerful, although there was just a hint of anxiety in her eyes. "This retreat is important for us."

"We have confidence in your capability," Mr. Warner said. "You've shown great skill in handling the children." Mr. Warner was not a person who used flattery, and I knew he was sincere.

Mr. and Mrs. Warner were going away to Suzhou for something they called a "retreat." I didn't know what they were retreating from, but I guessed it had something to do with their religion. Mr. Warner said missionaries had regular retreats and always returned to their duties refreshed in spirit.

Mr. Warner's trust in me wasn't complete, however. "Just in case anything happens," he added, "the houseboy knows what to do. He's been running things for a long time."

After Mr. and Mrs. Warner left, I waited for the two children to test my authority by seeing how far they could go. At least that was what I would have done under the circumstances.

"Our parents are having a vacation, so can we have one, too?" asked Grace. "We can skip lessons for a couple of days."

Since this was exactly what I was expecting, I had my answer ready. "Your parents are not having a vacation. They are having a retreat. That's quite a different thing."

I suspected that the children were as ignorant as I was about what a retreat was. Grace gave only a token struggle, proving that I was right. I waited for further resistance from Billy, always the more obstinate and ingenious of the two. But he surprised me by not raising any objections at all.

The first day passed peacefully enough. I was able to read a passage from a book on English history to Grace without interruption from Billy. When his turn came to work with me, he quietly recited the words he had been assigned to learn. Since he was a quick child, I wasn't surprised that he had learned the words. What surprised me was his toneless voice as he read them.

The next day began in the same quiet way, without Billy's usual attempts to disrupt the lessons. At lunchtime, he ate hardly any of the meatballs, usually a favorite of his.

Seeing that he looked tired, I suggested a nap, and to my amazement, he agreed. Even Grace's mouth dropped open at the sight of her brother going obediently upstairs to his room.

不
要
纏
足

Late in the afternoon, when I tiptoed into his room, he was still asleep. It was not a restful sleep, however. He tossed around and made soft little grunts. I felt his forehead and gasped. Billy was burning with fever.

"He's sick, isn't he?" whispered Grace, who was standing by the door.

"Yes, we have to do something right away!" I replied. But what? I thought of Grandmother and Father, and for an instant I was overcome with panic. I had already lost two people dear to me. I couldn't let Billy die, too!

At the sight of Grace's white, frightened face, I forced myself to be calm. Rushing downstairs, I called the houseboy. "Master Billy is very sick!" I took a moment to steady my voice, knowing I couldn't afford to show panic. "We need a doctor. Do you know of a good one?"

The houseboy frowned. "Mr. and Mrs. Warner always called their own doctor. He's an American, and I don't know the name."

The houseboy probably couldn't remember the name even if he had heard it, I thought. Western names were hard to pronounce, much less recall.

I tried to think what would have been done at my own home. The Tao family doctor was a prominent expert in Chinese medicine, but everyone referred to him as simply Master Physician, and I had never heard his name mentioned.

Shushing Grace, who was gulping and trying to control her sobs, I thought furiously. I could go home and ask Mother for the name of the doctor. I had money that the Warners had paid me, and I could hire a rickshaw. "I'm going out for a doctor," I told the houseboy. "Please order a rickshaw for me."

The houseboy looked at me for a moment. "Yes, Miss Tao," he said. "I will find one right away."

It wasn't until my rickshaw was halfway down the street that I realized the houseboy had addressed me as Miss Tao. But there was no time to savor this small triumph.

Nanjing was not a large city, and the ride from the Warners' to my home couldn't have taken more than fifteen minutes. But it felt like hours.

I felt my heart beat faster as the rickshaw turned into the familiar street and drew up at the gate. The rickshaw man knocked on the gate, and I climbed out, my legs feeling weak.

When the grizzled gatekeeper opened the door, I took a deep breath. "Lao Wang, do you remember me?"

The gatekeeper gaped at me. "Miss Three?" he said hoarsely.

"I need a doctor, Lao Wang," I said. "Is my mother home?"

The gatekeeper shook his head. "She has gone to visit Miss Two—only I have to remember that she's Mrs. Chen now. But the master is home. Shall I tell him you're here?"

The last thing I wanted was to ask Big Uncle for help. I decided to go to Second Sister's home, where Mother was. Either Mother or Second Sister would be able to help me.

I had never visited Second Sister's new home with the Chens. It was only about ten minutes away, but again the ride seemed to take hours.

The rickshaw man drew up at an unfamiliar gate and knocked on the door. When the gatekeeper opened the door and saw me, he glared. I was shocked by the hostility in his eyes. "We don't have anything to do with foreigners here!" he snarled, and banged the gate in my face.

I was too stunned to move. Finally the rickshaw man coughed. "Shall we try another place, young miss?"

Slowly I climbed back into the rickshaw. How could that gatekeeper mistake me for a foreigner? Then I realized that I was dressed entirely in Western clothes. But surely the man could tell from my features that I was Chinese! Perhaps he had never seen a foreigner before and judged only by my clothes.

Suddenly I wanted to cover my face and weep. At the Warners', I was a Chinese and a heathen. At Second Sister's home, I was turned away as a foreigner.

I looked at the blank mud-colored walls on both sides of the street, a sight familiar to me since childhood. I had once lived a pampered life inside such walls. Now I was on the outside of the walls.

Again the rickshaw driver coughed. "Shall I take you back, young miss?" he asked.

This was no time for self-pity. Billy was very sick and needed my help. Very well. Since the Chens' gatekeeper regarded me as a foreigner, I would go to a foreigner for help. I gave the rickshaw man Miss Gilbertson's address.

School was over for the day, and my old teacher was at home. After one look at my face, she put her arms around me. "What can I do to help?" she asked.

Now that I no longer had to act like an adult, I broke down and cried. "You must be tired of listening to me cry every time I see you."

"You don't cry all the time," said Miss Gilbertson. "Sometimes you read English to me, and you read beautifully."

As she reached for a handkerchief, I shook my head and brought out her old one from my pocket. "See, I still have the first one."

After wiping my eyes, I told Miss Gilbertson about Billy's high fever. "The Warners go to an American doctor," I said. "Do you know his name?"

It seemed that Miss Gilbertson and many of the other foreigners in Nanjing went to the same doctor. "I'll take you to him right away," she said.

Billy's illness turned out to be measles, and by the time I arrived back with the doctor, spots had already appeared on his face. The servants at the Warners' were alarmed by the red spots, thinking they might be a sign of smallpox. After the doctor had made his diagnosis, I reassured them that that

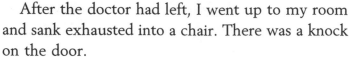
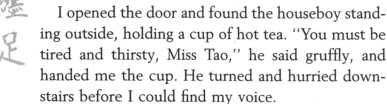

was not the case. I had already had measles myself, as had most of the staff.

After the doctor had left, I went up to my room and sank exhausted into a chair. There was a knock on the door.

I opened the door and found the houseboy standing outside, holding a cup of hot tea. "You must be tired and thirsty, Miss Tao," he said gruffly, and handed me the cup. He turned and hurried downstairs before I could find my voice.

Miss Gilbertson telephoned Mr. and Mrs. Warner about Billy, and they hurried back early from Suzhou. By the time they burst through the door, the house was calm and everything was under control.

Although she was not a demonstrative person, Mrs. Warner hugged me. "My dear, I'm so impressed by your initiative! We were lucky to have found you for our children."

My relationship with the houseboy improved. He was the only adult in the house I could really talk to, since Mr. and Mrs. Warner were busy and away most of the day. Like me, the houseboy often faced the clash of two cultures, and I got a lot of useful advice from him.

I should have been proud and happy. But in the days that followed Billy's illness, I couldn't forget the hatred on the face of the Chens' gatekeeper as he closed the door in my face. I felt like an exile in Nanjing, the city of my birth.

110

With the deaths of Grandmother and Father, I had lost the only people who gave me support at home. And yet things could have been worse. I had found refuge among the foreigners.

If, by a miracle, Big Uncle ever allowed me to return home, would I be able to regain my position in Chinese society and become a daughter of the Taos again? I didn't think so.

Once, when I was a small child running away from my amah, I had skipped into the kitchen garden. The cook had shown me a clump of bamboo. Only the tiny tips were showing. "Look, these shoots are good to eat," he had said, pushing some sand aside and uncovering two small plants. "They're still tender."

I saw another bunch of bamboo shoots, poking like green spearheads out of the ground. "What about those shoots over there?"

"They're too tough to eat," said the cook. "They've been outside in the air and sun."

"What if I cover them with sand?" I asked. "Will that make them tender again?"

The cook laughed. "No, it's too late. Once they've become tough, nothing will make them soft again."

I realized that I was like a bamboo shoot that had been outside in the air and sun. I could never again be like my sisters and other delicate Chinese girls with bound feet who spent their days in an inner chamber. I was too tough now.

不
要
纏
足

* * *

When Mr. Warner called me into his library again, I
had a good idea of what he was about to say. From
hints dropped by Mrs. Warner and the children, I
already knew that the family was going back to
America soon. Missionaries received something
called a furlough every few years. It was a kind of
vacation and allowed them to spend one year in
their own home. The Warners would be leaving
Nanjing and going back to their home in San Francisco.

I would miss the children very much, for I had
grown to love them like family. I knew Billy better
than I knew my own little brother, since Billy's care
had been in my hands, whereas Little Brother had
had his own amah to look after him.

Now I had to find another job. Perhaps the Warners could recommend me to other Americans. During my three years with them, my English had
improved beyond measure. Sometimes visitors,
overhearing me speak, took me for an American. I
had also grown greatly not only in height, but also
in confidence. I was sure I could cope with the children in another family, however difficult.

But I had guessed wrong about what Mr. Warner
was going to say. He folded his hands and looked at
me almost nervously. "Eileen, Mrs. Warner and I
have talked things over, and we'd like to make a
proposal to you: Would you consider going to
America with us?"

Too surprised to speak, I could only stare at him.

When I finally found my voice, the only thing I could think of saying was, "Is Billy being difficult again?"

Mr. Warner laughed, and I blushed at the tactlessness of my remark. Then Mr. Warner sobered. "Actually, there is some truth in what you said. When we told the children that we were going back to America, the first thing they asked was whether you would be coming with us."

I was so deeply touched that again I found myself unable to speak. Mr. Warner spared me the need to reply and went on. "When we return to San Francisco, Grace will be starting third grade and Billy the second. You're right that he is the one who presents a problem."

I rushed to defend Billy. "I'm sure he's as well prepared as any of the other children in school. His mind is very quick."

"That's not what worries us," said Mr. Warner. "Billy has learned his letters and even some words. He's ahead of other children his age in that respect. The trouble is that he is immature socially. You must know from firsthand experience that he can be obstinate. We think it best to continue teaching him at home until we return to Nanjing."

I began to see what Mr. Warner was driving at. "You want me to come with you and continue to look after him?"

Mr. Warner nodded. "Both children will have a lot of adjusting to do after their years in China. Their social life here has been too narrow for them to learn how to behave around other children. Having you with us will make the transition far less painful for them."

My thoughts were in turmoil, and I did not reply immediately. Mr. Warner said, "I know that we're asking you to make a great personal sacrifice in leaving your country and crossing the ocean to go all the way to America."

After a moment he added, with some difficulty and embarrassment, "Miss Gilbertson has told us a little of your history. We've also noticed that you have not had contact with your family. That was why we thought you might consider coming with us."

"I'd like to think things over," I said finally. "May I give you my answer tomorrow?"

But as I mounted the stair to my room, I already knew what my answer would be.

I took the rickshaw to the Tao family residence for the last time.

Lao Wang, the gatekeeper, told me Mother was home. But before visiting my mother, I went to see my uncle. I wanted to make the unpleasant visit first, to get it over with.

Big Uncle looked much older. His once-full cheeks were droopy, so that he seemed to have dewlaps. Now that he had no power over me, I found him almost pathetic. He was still elegantly dressed in a long silk robe, and the china teacup he held in his hand was the usual exquisite egg-shell porcelain. But he no longer had his former fire.

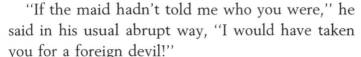

"If the maid hadn't told me who you were," he said in his usual abrupt way, "I would have taken you for a foreign devil!"

"I'd have to have a much longer nose," I retorted.

"At least you haven't lost your impudence!" said Big Uncle. He took a sip of tea. "Well, you have condescended to visit us at last. To what do we owe this honor?"

I could be abrupt, too. "I'm leaving China and going to America."

Slowly and carefully Big Uncle put his teacup down. The expression on his face was one I had never seen there before. I could only describe it as a mixture of guilt, regret, and even admiration. "It's been years since you've allowed me to have any influence on your actions. I'm surprised that you even bother to come and tell me."

"Since you are the head of the family, I thought you should be informed," I said.

Big Uncle's smile was twisted. "Head of the family? So you admit it finally?"

I regarded him thoughtfully. "I don't think you would have carried out your threat to make me go to the Fengs as a concubine or send me to a nunnery. You have too much pride in the Tao family name."

不
要
纏
足

"It seems that I have underestimated you," said Big Uncle. "Why did you really come today?"

"I wanted to say good-bye to my family, since I may never see any of you again," I replied.

"Your brother is not home," Big Uncle said. "He is going to a public school."

At the news I felt a mixture of joy and bitterness: joy, because despite his violent disapproval of public schools, Big Uncle had respected Father's wishes; bitterness, because there was not enough money to pay tuition for *me*, a mere girl, but there was enough to pay for my brother.

Suddenly I knew what I would do. I had my pay from the Warners in my pocket, and in three years I had spent hardly any of it. I took out the heavy bag. "You told me how tight finances were in the Tao family. You'd better take this to help with my brother's education." I placed the money on Big Uncle's table, and the *clink* made by the coins in the bag sounded sweet in my ears.

Without waiting for his answer, I walked out of his study and went to see Mother. I couldn't resist a swagger—which was possible because I didn't have to hobble on bound feet.

Unlike Big Uncle, Mother hardly seemed to have aged at all. Her hair was still jet black and her face unlined. "Too bad Little Brother isn't home to see you, Ailin," she said tearfully. "You should have warned us you were coming!"

"Big Uncle told me Little Brother is going to a public school," I said. I wondered if I would recognize Little Brother now. He certainly wouldn't recognize *me* in a Western dress!

"He's going to the same public school that Liu Hanwei went to," said Mother. She stole a glance at me. "Did you know that Hanwei won a government scholarship to go study in America?"

At the mention of Hanwei, I found that I felt no ache for my loss. He was nice enough and would probably make an easy husband to manage. But I didn't regret not marrying him. "Maybe I'll even run into him in America," I said lightly.

Mother burst into a storm of weeping. "Oh, Ailin, I've failed in my duty as a mother! I should have been stronger and insisted on having your feet bound!"

Now I finally understood why so many generations of mothers kept the custom of binding their daughters' feet. They believed that their primary duty in raising a daughter was to have her marry well, and the girl was considered attractive and marriageable only if she had bound feet.

"I never thought it would come to this!" sobbed Mother. "I knew you were headstrong, but you don't deserve this terrible fate! You will be living in a country filled with foreign devils!"

I had always thought that Mother loved only Little Brother and my two sisters, who gave her so much less trouble than I did. The only time she spoke to me was to correct or scold me. Now I realized that she loved me, too.

"Mother, I've been living in a house filled with

foreign devils for almost three years!" I said. "I'm strong enough to stand it!"

I was no delicate shoot buried in the sand. I was a stalk of bamboo, strong enough to stand against wind and snow.

CHAPTER
TEN

The biggest boat I had ever traveled on had been a ferry across the Yangtze River. And now I was boarding an ocean liner that would cross the Pacific Ocean. At the Shanghai docks I was just one of hundreds of passengers struggling to go up the gangplank. In my excitement I didn't have time to feel any pangs at leaving China.

I didn't realize at first that I was being put in the third-class section of the ship. The Warners were traveling second-class, and the steward was the one who told me that my cabin was in a level below theirs. I followed him down, down, and down narrow, winding stairs.

"We must be close to the bottom of the boat," I said nervously.

He laughed. "The steerage level is even lower."

He stopped in a dark, narrow corridor and pointed at a door. "Here's your cabin."

I entered a cabin containing four upper and four lower bunks. It seemed that I would be sharing the space with seven other people. I had never slept in a room with strangers before, but then everything about the boat was utterly alien. This was just another stage in the changing of my world.

After stowing away my luggage, I went back on deck. There were so many people milling around that I almost gave up hope of finding the Warners again. Maybe I wouldn't see them until we arrived in America!

But I did manage to find them eventually, helped by the sound of the children's voices. I saw Grace and Billy on the second-class deck, peering over the railing and yelling to some friends on the dock. They were beside themselves with excitement.

When Mrs. Warner saw me, she looked acutely embarrassed. "You mustn't misunderstand, Eileen. It's not that we don't respect you. If we could possibly afford it, we'd put you together with the children, or even get you a separate stateroom. But Mr. Warner's salary simply doesn't cover the cost of another second-class passage."

I was not offended, but I *was* surprised. By now I knew the Warners wouldn't do anything intentionally to demean me. What I hadn't realized was that they were far from rich. In China they could afford a houseful of servants, including a live-in tutor for their children. Aboard an American ship they were only second-class passengers.

I was almost as embarrassed as my employer and did my best to answer calmly. "Don't worry, Mrs. Warner. My cabin is quite clean and comfortable. Besides, the voyage won't last forever."

Mrs. Warner opened her mouth to reply but was called away to greet some acquaintances who had come to say good-bye. Watching Grace and Billy waving to friends, I felt a lump in my throat. I began to wave vigorously at a total stranger below. I had to show the Warners that there were friends coming to see me off, too.

To my amazement I noticed that someone was actually waving back and shouting my name. A plump, short figure pushed forward and ran up the gangplank. It was Xueyan!

"I thought I'd never see you again!" she cried, thrusting herself through the crowd at the railing. Tears were streaming down her face.

I had seen Xueyan only once during my three years with the Warners, and that was at Miss Gilbertson's party. Occupied with Grace and Billy, I had been too busy to visit Xueyan at her home. Also, it had been painful to know that she was continuing her studies at the school while I had to go to work.

But now I was overcome at seeing my friend. I finally managed to clear my throat. "You've cut your hair."

不
要
纏
足

"Is that all you can say?" Xueyan cried. "After all the trouble I took to find you?"

When we finished mopping our eyes, Xueyan said she had heard from Miss Gilbertson that I was leaving for America and had wanted to see me one last time. She had gone to my home and found out from Mother the name of my ship and the date of departure. She had come all the way to Shanghai by train from Nanjing, a journey of several hours.

A loud toot interrupted our talk and made us jump. "I'd better get off the ship, or I might wind up going with you to America," said Xueyan.

"Well, why not?" I said. I even managed a smile.

Xueyan's lips quivered. "How I envy you! You're embarking on a great adventure!"

Of course Xueyan was only trying to cheer me up, I thought. Then I realized that she was perfectly sincere. I felt my spirits begin to lift. We promised each other to write, and it lifted my spirits even further to realize that I would have many exciting things to write about.

As Xueyan started down the gangplank, she suddenly turned back. "I almost forgot! In fact this was one of the reasons for coming." She took a pouch from her pocket and handed it over. It was the bag of money I had put on Big Uncle's table. "Your uncle told me he was afraid you might wind up in some hole aboard the ship. He wanted to make sure that you'd have accommodations suitable for a daughter of the Tao family."

* * *

Our ship skirted the edge of a typhoon, which made it toss violently. I had an upper bunk, and I was afraid I'd fall out in spite of the railing. Soon I became too seasick to care. It didn't help that the cabin was filled with the smell of vomit and the moans of those who wanted to die.

By the fourth day the waves calmed, and when my death wish had passed, I finally staggered up on deck. Again, I had to go up flights of stairs and meander around mazelike corridors before I found the Warners in the second-class lounge.

The children yelled with delight to see me again. Billy hurled himself so violently at me that I was knocked down, and the two of us rolled around on the floor, laughing hysterically.

During the voyage I spent most of the day in second class with the Warners and returned to the third-class section only for meals and at bedtime. I didn't even try to use the money from Big Uncle to change my stateroom. It would humiliate my employers. Besides, I had no idea of how to go about getting a cabin in a higher class.

It was true that descending into the third-class section after the fresh air on deck was an ordeal. There was little ventilation down in the bowels of the ship, and nowhere could I escape the miasma of unwashed bodies and cooking smells. But as I had said to Mrs. Warner, the voyage wouldn't last forever. The blow to my status was nothing new. I had endured worse.

Only on one occasion did I feel humiliated. Billy

could not get used to the way that the time for meals was advanced every day. The ship was heading east, and that meant the clock had to be regularly set forward. He was never hungry when the dinner gong rang, and he couldn't eat like the adults, who took advantage of the opportunity to gorge themselves. Billy would eat only a little at the table and then get hungry between meals. Once, he complained so pitifully that I went into the snack bar of the lounge in search of some food for him.

The bartender at the counter looked at me coldly. "Aren't you a third-class passenger?"

I admitted that I was. "I need a cookie for a little boy I look after."

"Go back down to the third-class section!" the bartender ordered curtly. "One of the waiters in the kitchen will find something suitable for you."

I felt the blood rush to my face. I took a deep breath, and without conscious effort, I spoke in the haughty tones of Miss Scott, my history teacher at the MacIntosh School. "If you had taken the trouble to ask, I could have told you that while I'm in the third class, the little boy is a second-class passenger. Now, will you provide me with some cookies suited to his station?"

The bartender's jaw dropped. Finally he blinked, reached up to a shelf, and silently handed me a packet of cookies. He was still staring as I walked to the door.

The sound of soft laughter made me look back. A young Chinese man, who had been sitting on a sofa, got up and walked over. He said something in Cantonese, which I didn't understand. So I shook my head and told him in English that I was from Nanjing and spoke only Mandarin.

He switched also to English. "I was just saying that you did a good job of putting that bartender in his place. He's Chinese but treats most Chinese customers like dirt. I had to call a steward to vouch for my right to sit in this chair. Where did you learn to speak English like that?"

He accompanied me back on deck, and I told him a little about the missionary school I had attended. I noticed that he glanced at my feet briefly and then tactfully looked away.

I learned that his name was James Chew and that he had been born in San Francisco, where his father owned a restaurant. He was just returning from a business trip to Canton, his ancestral home. Like many southerners I had met, he had rounder eyes than the northerners. Southerners also tend to be slight in build, but James Chew was tall and on the husky side. Maybe growing up in America and breathing American air had made him bigger.

I found it pleasant to chat with him, although he was about ten years older than I was. That made him around twenty-six. In spite of his advanced age, he seemed very interested in my background and asked many questions about the Warners and the MacIntosh School.

The rest of the voyage was pleasant. The Pacific, called *Taiping Yang* by the Chinese, lived up to its name as the "Sea of Peace" and stayed calm. I loved looking at the purple waves, the flying fish, and the incredibly brilliant stars at night. I ran into James Chew quite a few times. In fact, he often took a walk on deck at the same time the children and I did.

James also showed us how to consult the bulletin board and keep track of the progress of our ship. When we crossed the international date line, he explained why it was necessary to set the calendar back one day.

There was a children's activity room on board, where a storyteller entertained the young people for an hour every afternoon. Since that freed me from keeping an eye on Grace and Billy, I was able to sit in a deck chair outside the activity room and read. Soon I began to find James Chew regularly sitting in the chair next to me.

"I hope you don't mind my prying," he said, spreading a lap robe over my knees, although it was quite warm. "You seem to be very well educated, and I'm wondering how you ended up taking care of a couple of American children." He added hurriedly, "There's nothing wrong with taking care of kids. It's an honest job. But didn't your family think all that money spent on education was wasted?"

"My family was the main reason why I wound up going to America," I began, and hesitated. Then I continued. "You must have noticed that I don't have bound feet."

He nodded. "Nobody in America has bound feet—except some women brought over as wives for wealthy Chinese businessmen."

"The Chinese women with unbound feet become servants or laborers, I suppose," I said dryly.

"Most do," James admitted.

He started to say something more, but Grace and Billy came out of the activity room and began telling me about the story they had just heard.

We settled into a daily routine. While Grace and Billy were in the children's activity room, James and I chatted outside on the deck. Talking to him was a bit like talking to Second Sister. He was someone who was ready to listen sympathetically without passing judgment.

He asked me again how I had wound up as a nanny for the Warners. Although I had known him for only a couple of weeks, I found myself confiding in him. Up to then Miss Gilbertson had been the only person who knew my full story. I hadn't even been able to confide completely in the Warners.

Before I knew it I began to tell James Chew about my family, about Father, Grandmother, and Big Uncle. I wanted him to know the truth. I even told him about my broken engagement.

"So that's my story," I concluded. "Now you know why I'm on a ship heading for America."

He stared at me for a long time. Finally he said, "You're the bravest person I've ever met."

At first I thought he was making fun of me. Then

I realized he was serious, and I found myself blushing furiously. "I don't know what you mean. I'm not a revolutionary or anything. I'm not a woman warrior, like Hua Mulan."

"You *are* a revolutionary," said James. "And I admire you for fighting a war, a war against tradition."

"So you don't think it's wrong to fight tradition?" I asked. Big Uncle believed that only by maintaining our traditions could we keep our cultural heritage. Father was the one who believed we should look to the new, as well as preserving the old.

"There are some traditions that we just have to fight," said James. He sounded so positive on this point that I wondered if it applied to something in his own life.

I was glad James agreed with Father. I was beginning to like James a lot, and I wanted to know more about him.

"I've told you a lot about my family," I said. "Now tell me about *your* family. How did they happen to go to America?"

He grinned. "My family isn't upper class like yours. Is that going to stop you from talking to me?"

I grinned back. "I'm not exactly in a position to talk about class. After all, I'm a third-class passenger, and I'm allowed here in second class only because I'm looking after Grace and Billy."

128

A steward walked by, and James asked him for two cups of beef tea. It didn't sound very appetizing. "I'm not sure I want tea that's made from beef," I said.

"It's not really tea," explained James. "It's a kind of soup, and it's served between meals on the boat. Some passengers think it helps settle their stomachs."

I found it strange to drink soup without anything solid to go with it, but I was willing to give it a try. The soup was rather salty, but the hot liquid felt good going down my throat.

As we sipped, James began to tell me about his family. "My grandfather went to California during the Gold Rush in 1849."

Jinshan, the Chinese name for San Francisco, meant "Golden Mountain," and I pictured gold rushing down the mountain in a stream. "Your grandfather must have become fabulously rich!"

James smiled wryly. "No such luck. Grandfather didn't manage to make a strike. Instead, he had the idea of opening a restaurant for the miners. It was very hard work, but in the end he did pretty well for himself."

"Well enough to bring his family over to America?" I asked.

"He went back to his hometown in Canton and got married to the girl his family had found for him," said James. "Poor girl, she had expected him to return to China loaded with bags of gold, build a big house for her, and hire lots of servants. Instead, Grandfather took her back to America to work her feet off in a restaurant."

I looked at James and at his well-cut suit. After my three years with the Warners I had seen enough Westerners and their clothes to be able to tell a well-cut suit from a poorly cut one. "Your grandfather's restaurant must have prospered."

James nodded. "The hard work paid off. My father inherited the restaurant, which continued to grow under his management."

"So your mother had an easier life, married to a successful restaurant owner," I said.

"No, she didn't," said James. "Some of the other wealthy Chinese businessmen in San Francisco arranged for wives to be sent to them from China, women with bound feet. But Father went back to China and married a country girl from his ancestral village."

I remembered my old wet nurse, a country woman with a broad lap, who comforted me and hugged me and crooned lullabies. James's father had made a good choice, I thought.

"Besides, women with bound feet have to stay indoors all day long," continued James. "Father didn't want a wife who spent her time drinking tea, eating watermelon seeds, and playing mahjongg. He wanted someone who would be able to walk out with him without being jeered at by Americans."

I sat up. "You mean Americans make fun of girls

with bound feet?'' This was an astounding idea to me. I was so used to being jeered at for having *unbound* feet.

"Some of the wives in Chinatown even try to hide the fact that they have bound feet,'' said James. "They wear big shoes and stuff the extra room with cotton. But they can't disguise the way they walk: They have to take tiny steps, and they sway from side to side.''

"For a thousand years the Chinese have prized that dainty, swaying walk,'' I murmured, picturing the way my grandmother, mother, and sisters walked. It was a sign of their status.

"Well, Americans have different tastes,'' said James.

"How do you personally feel about it?'' I asked. "Do you think like an American or like most Chinese?'' It suddenly became important for me to know.

"I feel the same way as my father,'' he said instantly. "When I marry, I want a companion, not a status symbol.''

I felt a rush of warmth at hearing his words and buried my nose in the steam from my cup of beef tea. After a minute I asked, "Will you take over from your father someday?'' The restaurant had to be doing good business if James could afford to travel to China—in second class.

James shook his head. "I'm a younger son, so that means my elder brother is taking over the restaurant, and I'm supposed to work under him.''

不
要
纏
足

I studied his face. "You don't look forward to working under him."

"Is it that obvious? No, I don't enjoy working under my brother. He's not a good businessman, and I hate seeing the restaurant going downhill in his hands."

"And it's impossible to pass the business over to a younger son," I murmured. Even if James's father preferred to marry a woman with unbound feet, he kept to the old traditional ways in some respects.

James didn't have a chance to answer because the door of the activity room opened and the children came spilling out. Grace and Billy said they were tired of sitting still for an hour and wanted me to take them for a walk. As I held the children's hands and walked with them around the ship, I thought about James Chew's family history.

"I understand you've found an admirer," Mrs. Warner said to me a couple of days later.

"Oh, you mean James Chew," I said casually. "He was nice to me when the bartender in the lounge tried to order me back to third class."

Mrs. Warner flushed. "I'm sorry, Eileen. I shall have to ask Mr. Warner to speak to the bartender."

"No, no, it turned out all right," I reassured her. "Anyway, James was in the lounge at the time, and that was how we got acquainted." Mrs. Warner continued to look uncomfortable, so I told her a little about James's family and background.

In Nanjing Mrs. Warner and I had seldom had a

chance to have a real conversation. After the crisis over Billy's measles, her manner to me had become much warmer, and she had made some attempts to talk with me. But like her husband, she was busy with her missionary work most of the day, while I spent my time with the children. Only during Sunday dinner were we all together.

Now, aboard the ship, I found out that she came originally from New England, which was way over on the eastern side of America, more than three thousand miles from San Francisco. Mr. Warner was from Iowa, a state in the middle of the country. The two of them had met when he went to college, and after they got married they moved west. When they both decided to become missionaries, they chose China as their field. They worked first in Shanghai and then were assigned by their mission to Nanjing.

I was impressed by all the moving the Warners had to do. For that matter, James's family had done some drastic moving, too. Truly, Americans were a people who moved around. And I thought *I* had taken a big step by going outside the Tao family compound.

Mrs. Warner seemed to grow increasingly nervous as the ship approached its destination. "Aren't you glad to be going home to San Francisco?" I asked.

Mrs. Warner hesitated. "It's hard to say exactly where home is for me," she said. "We've been in China for so many years that both Grace and Billy have gotten used to the life there. Billy, in fact, thinks of America as a foreign country. I don't know how he will take to living in San Francisco."

I tried to imagine what it was like for the Warners, who went home only once every seven years on furloughs. The life chosen by the missionaries was not an easy one. Whether or not I agreed with their religious beliefs, I had to admire them for their hard work and dedication.

James Chew also seemed sorry that the voyage was drawing to a close. "This trip might be my last one for a while," he said. "It was my idea. I suggested to my father that by going back to Canton, I could arrange for our suppliers to sell directly to our restaurant."

"You can't buy the supplies for your restaurant in America?" I asked.

"We need all sorts of spices and ingredients not available in America," he explained. "We've always had to go through a lot of middlemen, and that raises the prices on everything."

I didn't know what *middlemen* meant, but what struck me were his words about this being his last trip. "You don't expect to do any more traveling?"

He sighed. "Not when my brother takes over the management of the restaurant. He and I have very different ideas about the business. My father has been sick for more than a year now, and he says he can't put off his retirement any longer."

"So what will you do?" I asked.

He sighed even more deeply. "I suppose I have to work under my brother, even if it means watching the business go to ruin." He turned and looked at me. "I hope we meet again in San Francisco. Do you know where you'll be staying?"

I shook my head. It had never occurred to me to ask the Warners for their address. "Maybe we'll run into each other. Is San Francisco a large city?"

"I'm afraid it's very large," replied James. "But please try to go to Chinatown and look for the Green Pavilion restaurant. It's on Dupont Street."

His eyes were very intent as he spoke. I wanted to promise him that I would find some way to visit his father's restaurant, but I suddenly felt shy and couldn't find anything to say.

James seemed to sense my embarrassment and adopted a lighter tone. "Look! Billy is hungry again. Why don't we badger the bartender for another snack?"

When land was finally sighted I stood on deck, holding Grace and Billy by the hand. All three of us were silent. I had entered a totally new world when I enrolled in the MacIntosh School, and another one when I went to live with an American family. Now I was about to enter still another new world—literally the New World.

CHAPTER
ELEVEN

The Warners' house in San Francisco was half-way up a hill. It was in a pleasant neighbor-hood on the northwest side of the city, and the view down to the ocean from the front windows was spectacular. The trees were permanently swept back by the sea breezes, and in the late afternoon the fog rolled over us like a wadded quilt. I couldn't stop marveling at the beauty of my surroundings. Nanjing was a flat city, with some pretty lakes and low hills in the outskirts. San Francisco, on the other hand, had sharp hills and a roaring ocean. The city—maybe all of America—seemed rugged and untamed.

It didn't take long for me to realize that the Warners were not well off. Their house, which had been rented while the family was in China, needed a thorough cleaning. After we arrived, I waited for a crew of servants to come and do the necessary work. I was shocked when Mr. and Mrs. Warner themselves took up brooms, mops, and dusters. Even their houseboy back in Nanjing would never use a broom or a mop. That was beneath his dignity.

I offered to help with the cleaning, but to my great relief Mrs. Warner preferred to have me keep the children busy and out of the way. I helped the children put away their belongings. I was sharing the bigger of the two upstairs bedrooms with Grace, while Billy had a tiny room facing the back of the house. It was hardly bigger than a closet.

By late afternoon Billy was whining with hunger. I was pretty hungry myself, since all we'd had for lunch had been some pieces of bread with butter. I tiptoed cautiously downstairs, hoping the cook would have some tidbits I could take up to Billy. I had done this often in Nanjing, and the cook had been willing to oblige me, although he was temperamental and surly toward the rest of the household.

The kitchen was very different from the one in the Warners' Nanjing house. The stove here didn't have a hole for resting the wok, and there was no roaring fire inside. There was no fire at all in the stove. In fact, there was not a soul in the kitchen.

I had to face the bitter truth: Not only did the Warners have no servants to do the cleaning, they had no cook to prepare the meals.

I heard the front door of the small house open, and Mrs. Warner, looking very disheveled, staggered

不要纏足

in with some parcels. She dropped them on the kitchen table and sank into a chair. For a moment she looked too tired to speak. Then she gave a great sigh. "I'd better start getting dinner ready. You know, I'm already homesick for Nanjing."

I pulled myself together. "*I'm* not. I think coming to America is a great adventure!" My employer needed support, and I tried to sound bracing. "You must be tired. Let me help with the cooking."

Mrs. Warner grinned. "My dear, have you ever done any cooking before?"

I had to admit that I hadn't. "But I can learn!"

"Well, at least I've cooked before," said Mrs. Warner. "I've been spoiled in China, but I can still remember a few basic things."

Mrs. Warner might still remember a few basic things about cooking, but she was badly out of practice. For the rest of my life I will never forget my first dinner at the Warners' house in San Francisco. The meal consisted of pork chops, boiled cabbage, and mashed potatoes. The cabbage was mashed, the potatoes were crunchy, and the pork chops tasted like scraps of lumber.

Billy was always the first to complain about food, but he took one look at his mother's rigid face and had the sense to say nothing. We all found it safer to say nothing. After the meal I got up to help Mrs. Warner clear the table. "Grace will help, too," Mrs. Warner said.

In the days that followed, I was not the only one

to find it hard adjusting to life in America. Mr. and Mrs. Warner, tight-lipped and overworked, spent little time at home. Grace had to enroll in a neighborhood school, but she didn't seem to feel the same joy that I had on entering my school. Eight-year-old Billy became so homesick for China that he started to behave like a four-year-old. I had to use all my ingenuity to keep him from throwing tantrums.

I did my best to help Mrs. Warner, for I felt closer to her now than I had in Nanjing. Although I had been hired to tutor the children, I didn't have the heart to sit back while she toiled so hard with the housework and cooking. I tried wielding a broom, but I didn't realize that I had to collect the dirt in a receptacle and deposit it in a refuse container. In China the maids simply swept everything out into the courtyard. I was no more successful with a mop, since I didn't know that for good results the mop had to be squeezed dry first.

One night, as I watched everyone around the dining table doggedly chewing away at Mrs. Warner's dinner, I was suddenly overcome by the desire to eat Chinese food. "Why don't I try to cook some rice?" I suggested. "Maybe I can also cut up some meat into shreds and stir-fry it with vegetables."

I was startled by the enthusiastic response from the whole Warner family. Grace clapped her hands, Billy jumped up from his seat in glee, and even Mr.

不
要
纏
足

Warner's solemn face broke into a grin. Mrs. Warner gave a great sigh. "I think that would be an excellent idea, Eileen."

That was how I began my career as a cook.

In China I had never set foot in the kitchen, but I had loved to prowl around the courtyard outside it, and I had seen the family chef wield his chopping knife. I knew about the quick "flash" style of cooking because I had seen the chef dump the finely sliced food into the hot wok and stir it around vigorously. Best of all, I knew how good food should taste.

Of course it took me a while to master even the most elementary techniques of cooking. Rice is the foundation of every Chinese meal, but it was surprisingly hard to cook well, I discovered. My first pot of rice turned out to be rice soup, but rice soup—called congee by some Westerners—was at least a recognized dish.

Mrs. Warner was so relieved at having some of the cooking taken off her hands that she was very patient with me. As my cooking gradually improved, the family stopped pretending to like my food. Their appreciation became genuine.

But it was hard work. I had never done so much physical labor before in my life. In addition to tutoring Billy and helping Grace with her work after school, I had to walk to a nearby store to shop for food and do an increasing amount of cooking.

Yet I had never felt so much self-satisfaction. True, I had been proud of my work at the MacIntosh School. True, I had been Grandmother's favorite. But Big Uncle had made it clear that a girl in a Chinese family was a luxury, someone who might be dearly loved but who was always a drain on the family resources. Girls didn't bring anything into a family. They were married off at great expense to some other family, where they fulfilled their duty by producing sons.

With the Warners, I felt I was making a contribution to the family. I was needed.

"I have to buy some soy sauce," I said.

Until that evening the Warners had held back from saying anything about my cooking. I knew perfectly well that they found it less than perfect, but they had not tried to criticize me. Maybe they were afraid I might resign from cooking and they would have to go back to mashed cabbage and wooden pork chops.

Billy, as usual, was the first one to speak his mind. "This doesn't taste like what we used to have," he said after a mouthful of my cabbage shreds stir-fried with chunks of beef.

The others tried to shush him, but it was too late. Besides, I agreed with him. My cooking, which came reasonably close to Chinese food in texture, had very little taste or color. It needed zing. For that, I needed certain ingredients, but none of the stores in our neighborhood had anything resembling Chinese groceries.

Suddenly I felt a tremendous hunger for long-

不
要
纏
足

grain rice, not the mushy kind used by Americans for making rice pudding. My mouth watered for soy sauce, for ginger, for bamboo shoots. . . .

"Maybe you can take Eileen to Chinatown, Imogene," Mr. Warner said. "She can find everything she needs there."

I caught my breath. James Chew had said something about his father's restaurant being in Chinatown. I had thought about James on and off, but like my family, Miss Gilbertson, and Xueyan, he had become a figure from the past. Now I felt a tingle of excitement at the possibility of seeing him again.

The very next morning Mrs. Warner took me by cable car to an entirely different part of San Francisco. Even before I got down from the cable car, I heard, saw, and smelled another world—a Chinese world. The street signs were written in Chinese characters. We got off on a street labeled *Douban Jie*. "This is Dupont Street," said Mrs. Warner, "the center of Chinatown."

I felt dazed as I stood on the sidewalk. I looked around at the vegetable stalls with bins containing all the familiar greens: bok choy, mustards, baby chrysanthemum leaves . . . I peered into the open storefronts and saw dried scallops, lotus stems, and bottles with Chinese writing on them.

"Why, what's the matter, Eileen?" asked Mrs. Warner. "Aren't you feeling well?"

That was when I realized that tears were streaming down my face. I was too overcome to speak, but finally mopped my eyes and managed to clear my throat. "It's like being back in China," I whispered.

For a moment it seemed that eight thousand miles of ocean no longer separated me from Nanjing, from the sweet-olive trees of the Tao residence, and from the faces of Mother, Second Sister, and Little Brother.

After that I went back alone to Chinatown once a week to buy the ingredients I needed. Sometimes it made me laugh to remember the days when Mother didn't even let me walk unaccompanied in the street and insisted that I go by rickshaw. Here in San Francisco I learned the right cable car to take so that I could make the trip myself.

I looked forward to these weekly trips. It was almost like returning to my own country, to my home. In Chinatown I was among people who looked just like me. I didn't feel like a foreigner there.

Only that wasn't quite true. Language was a problem, I found out immediately. When I picked up a bunch of greens and asked for the price in Mandarin, the shopkeeper didn't understand me and answered in Cantonese. The two of us ended up speaking English to communicate.

A good ear had always been my greatest asset. If I could learn English, I could certainly learn Cantonese. By my third visit, I could manage a few phrases.

"I need a lighter soy sauce," I was saying to a shopkeeper. "This one is too black."

"I think you have to say *sheng chou*," said a familiar voice behind me.

I spun around and saw James Chew. "But your pronunciation is pretty good," he added, smiling.

Although I had half hoped to meet him every time I came to Chinatown, I was surprised at how delighted I felt to see him at last. The only thing I could think of saying was, "Do you live around here?"

"My father's restaurant, the Green Pavilion, is just over there on the next block," he replied. "If you have time, how about coming over for some *dim sum*?"

I had never been inside a restaurant in my life. Eating with total strangers was not for well-born young women, and Mother would be shocked at the very idea. But of course, I had already eaten in the huge dining room of the ship, with hundreds of strangers. And times were changing, even in China.

Besides, I was nearly sixteen, old enough to make my own decisions. Nevertheless, I still felt a guilty thrill as I agreed to accompany James to his father's restaurant.

It was very noisy and crowded, with serving people rushing about like madmen. As the son of the proprietor, James was able to get a quiet table in a corner. We sat down, and I told him the reason for my trips to Chinatown. It was difficult to talk because I couldn't stop gobbling down the delectable food that kept arriving at our table.

144

I tried to make light of my attempts at cooking and my failures. Since the restaurant was so noisy, I wasn't even sure James could hear me very well. I certainly couldn't understand more than one word in three of his replies. But I could read the expression on his face. It was admiration.

Love and affection I had received lavishly from Father, Grandmother, and Second Sister. But admiration was different. Admiration was closer to respect, as from one adult to another.

The food was wonderful, but I was stuffed. When the next dish of steamed dumplings arrived, I waved it aside. "I can't eat another bite."

James nodded. "Let's go outside. It's too noisy in here."

"Thank you for a wonderful treat," I said as we emerged into the street. "I have to get back to the Warners'."

As we walked to the cable-car stop, James suddenly stopped and looked at me. "For the past few months I've been trying to decide about my future," he said slowly. "I don't like the way my brother is running the restaurant, but I couldn't find the nerve to break free. Meeting you like this has helped me to make up my mind."

I found my face growing warm. "What do you mean?"

James's eyes were very bright. "You left your family and took a position as a nanny because you refused to give up your independence."

不
要
纏
足

"You mean you might leave your family, too? Even work as a servant?" I was dismayed. I didn't want to be responsible for such a move.

"Even while slaving for a foreign family in a foreign country, you managed to keep your self-respect. That's what made me come to a decision. I've decided to start my own restaurant!"

Something close to fear made my heart beat faster. "I don't want the responsibility! I'm not the one who makes up your mind!"

James grinned. He looked younger, even mischievous. "But you *are* the one, whether you meant to be or not, and if I go bankrupt and lose my savings, it will all be your fault!"

We both laughed. "When can I see you again?" James asked when we heard the clang of the cable car approaching.

"Well, I usually shop here once a week," I replied. Then I added softly, "I can make it a definite time every Wednesday morning, say, at eleven?"

"I've made my decision," I told Mr. Warner. "I'm not returning to China with you. I'm staying in America."

"My dear, are you sure?" asked Mrs. Warner. "I can't help thinking that you're very young to be making such a very serious decision."

I had to hide a smile. I had made other serious decisions, and at an even earlier age. "Don't worry, Mrs. Warner. I know my own mind."

146

"Aren't you anxious to see your family again?" asked Mrs. Warner. "I know you've not been on close terms with them, but don't you want to see your mother and your brother and sisters? If you stay, it might be a long time before you get a chance to go back."

Mrs. Warner had put her finger on the hardest thing about my decision: my family. It might be years before I could feel Second Sister's comforting arms around me again. I wouldn't be able to talk to Little Brother about his public school. I might not see him grow up.

"May I ask you to bring these English books to my younger brother?" I said. I wanted to send Little Brother some toy trains, but realized that he might be too old for them. The sad thing was that I didn't know what sort of toy he enjoyed. Books would always be welcome, I thought.

Mrs. Warner cleared her throat. "Would you like us to bring some message to your family?"

I had corresponded with Miss Gilbertson and Xueyan but not directly with my family. Something had held me back. Although I was not ashamed of my position in the Warner family, I was afraid my relatives might not feel the same way about one of their members' working as a nanny. So I just shook my head. "I'll write to my family someday."

Mr. Warner continued to look grave. "We've met James Chew, and he seems like a responsible young man. We'll be honored to give you away at your wedding. But you haven't known him that long. Have you considered the fact that after we leave, you will have no other protector?"

"I've considered it," I said.

"And helping him run his restaurant!" said Mrs. Warner. "That's backbreaking work!"

Again I hid a smile. I knew a lot about hard work, from taking care of Grace and Billy and from cooking for the Warners right here in San Francisco. But all I said was, "Don't worry, I'm prepared to work hard."

Actually, James had said the same thing when he proposed marriage. "I'm not offering you an easy life. You'll be working much harder than you've ever done before."

And I had said, "I'm prepared." Then I added shyly, "If you need money to start your restaurant, I have a little bit saved up that you can have."

He laughed when I told him about the money my uncle had returned, and about my pay from the Warners, which I had carefully saved. "I'm afraid that to start a restaurant, we need more money than that—a lot more."

But he seemed deeply touched by my offer. He seized me in a fierce grip and kissed me hard.

EPILOGUE

As the details of my life flashed before me, I was almost startled by Hanwei's voice. "Why didn't you wait, Ailin? Why did you run away to that American family?" That was Hanwei's question.

His eyes were full of regret and reproach. "Things are changing in China," he said. "And more and more of my parents' friends are leaving their daughters' feet unbound. If you had waited, we could have gotten married, and you'd be leading a much easier life."

"An easier life as what?" I asked. I wasn't being sarcastic. I really wanted to know.

"Well . . ." He wasn't prepared for my question. "Well, as any upper-class wife, I suppose . . . you know, you'd be living like my mother, your mother. . . ."

I thought of my mother's life of ease. I thought

of Big Uncle's two wives. Of course, Hanwei wouldn't browbeat me like Big Uncle, but what would there be for me to do all day?

Did I ask that question aloud? Perhaps Hanwei read my mind, because he answered. "You could have become an English teacher. Some schools now have Chinese women teachers. Wasn't that your ambition?"

"No, I can never become a teacher," I said slowly, and for a moment I felt keen regret. "I never finished school."

"You could have gone back to Nanjing, at least!" cried Hanwei. "Instead, you stayed on in America! I can't bear the thought of all the work you've had to do!"

He was right about that. I did have to work hard. Some of the wives in Chinatown, those with bound feet who were married to wealthy businessmen, led lives of ease, shut up in their upstairs rooms. I knew I would lose my mind if I had to spend my days like that. I had chosen a different life.

Starting the restaurant with James had been truly backbreaking work during the first two years. He had warned me about the hardship, but it had been even worse than I had expected.

It was only recently that things had improved. Now James and I could afford to hire help, and we occasionally found opportunities to go out by ourselves to the zoo or take the ferry to the East Bay. I even had time to sit and chat with a guest about old times.

Seated across the table from Hanwei, I looked down at my work-worn hands. My fingers would never regain their slenderness and delicate tips. In comparison, Hanwei's hands were still the soft, pampered hands of someone who never had to rinse his socks, much less wash huge stacks of dishes day after day.

Suddenly I knew that I was ready at last to communicate with my family again. I wanted them to know exactly what my life was like. "Hanwei, can you take a message from me to my mother? And tell her all about this restaurant?"

He looked at me. "You don't mind if I tell them how hard you've had to work?"

"I'm proud of the hard work I did because by standing on my own two feet, I helped my husband make this restaurant a success," I said. I thought of the people who loved me. I knew my father would have been proud of me. I laughed and added, "By standing on my two *big* feet."

A Note on the Chinese Tradition
of Foot Binding

The practice of foot binding in China began around the end of the Tang Dynasty, or about 900 A.D. According to a popular legend, a dancing girl at the court of the Tang emperor bound her feet so that she could dance on her toes, somewhat like a ballet dancer. She was so graceful that many dancers imitated her, and the practice spread to court ladies and other aristocratic women.

Most historians, however, do not believe that the Tang Dynasty ladies had bound feet, because in sculpture and paintings they are generally shown as robust, even athletic. Polo was a popular sport among high-born women of the Tang era.

It wasn't until the Song Dynasty (960–1279) that there were definite records of women's having their feet bound. At first the practice was confined to aristocratic women, but gradually it spread to other classes of society. Peasant women and those who had to do hard physical labor escaped foot binding because it would have crippled them and made it impossible for them to move around efficiently.

In spite of the fact that foot binding was an excruciatingly painful process and rendered the victim useless as an active worker, the practice continued for more than a thousand years. Why did women allow themselves to suffer this procedure? The reason given was that men found bound feet attractive.

Chinese women, to be sure, were not the only ones who suffered agonies to attract men. Victorian women wore corsets so tight that they swooned at the slightest excitement. African women stretched their lips as big as plates or endured female circumcision. Some American women wear four-inch-high heels that force them to totter around.

I won't go into why high heels, tiny waists, or plate-sized lips are attractive to men. My aim is to try to understand why Chinese men were so entranced by women with feet less than three inches long. Photographs of these naked, crippled feet are a sickening sight. So what was the attraction?

There are a couple of theories. One is that having crippled feet makes a woman helpless and unable to run away, and some men are excited by the thought of helpless women.

But this does not explain everything. Not all Chinese men were sadists who enjoyed the idea of women in pain and at their mercy. The other theory is that it gave a man status to be able to afford a wife who could not work. It showed he was rich enough to support a "trophy" wife.

By the early years of the twentieth century, the practice finally began to die out, although among the upper classes women with bound feet were still preferred. Even today you can find a few isolated cases in China of old women with bound feet. They are ashamed of their feet, but they cannot remove the strips of bandages and wear normal shoes because it's too painful to walk without the support of the bindings.

It wasn't until the 1930s that the practice stopped more or less completely and mothers allowed their daughters' feet to go unbound. In some isolated areas, however, the practice went on until the 1940s! I met a woman in a small village who had bound feet, and she was in her fifties.

—*Lensey Namioka*